Out of the Mist: An Outer Banks Mystery

By Jayne Conrad Harding

Copyright

Cover photograph by Amanda Harding © 2011

Dedicated to Gary, Amanda, Ash, and Tyler, who also love the Outer Banks, and to Lee Barron, for her endless encouragement and help.

Thank you to Elena Gilly, Demi Emmanouil, Candy Dawson, and Janet Shackleford, for your encouragement and help. Also, to Tyler Ryals for his technical advice and expertise, and to Mandy Wren, who knows and loves horses.

I couldn't have done this without you!

Table of Contents

Chapter One

The sun sets early in late October. Darkness had fallen by the time that 11-year-old Kate, along with her mother, Zoe, and German shepherd, named Woolf, pulled their Jeep up behind a Range Rover whose tail lights glowed like red beacons in the deepening mist. The Rover clung closely to a wide place at the edge of the otherwise deserted road. Straight ahead and not far away lay sand and the Atlantic Ocean, where white-capped waves shone dimly beneath a cloud-dense sky, which neither stars nor moon were able to penetrate this night.

A man stepped out of the Range Rover into the darkness, and hurried to where they sat waiting. Zoe lowered her window, allowing the strong, wet wind to penetrate the artificial warmth in which the little family sat. Kate pulled up the hood of her coat and grasped the neck together, more tightly.

The man, the man her mother worked for to be exact, spoke impatiently. "Put it into four-wheel drive and let's get going. You're late and the tide is coming in." He turned away and then abruptly turned back. "Wait—I want you to stay close behind me while we do this. If we're going to make it at all, we have to leave right now."

Zoe opened her mouth to reply, but the man, Robert, raised his hand in a dramatically dismissive gesture. "Save it—it'll just have to wait. Come on—now!"

He returned to the Rover and both vehicles moved forward, pausing only to switch into four-wheel drive. Then, with Zoe following, they slid onto the cold sand, slithered down a short hill, veered to the left, and began their slow progression along the beach. No road lay ahead of them. There was only sand, and the remnants of a petrified cypress forest firmly planted in the waves. Those waves, Kate and Zoe noticed, were steadily reaching farther and farther across their own path and towards a sand dune-barrier on their left.

Robert was right; the tide was sweeping in quickly and Kate could see, even in the darkness, that the sea was rough and she was suddenly frightened. Woolf sat close beside her and she threw her arms around his neck and buried her face in the warmth of his comforting fur, as she had done whenever she was afraid, for as long as she could remember. However, at this moment, he also sensed danger and a combined growl and whimper emerged from his throat.

Neither spoke, in fact they hardly dared to even breathe, as Zoe tensely and carefully maneuvered the Jeep closely behind the Rover and the swiftly-moving water. At one point, they felt the Jeep lift off the sand and momentarily float before the tide pulled back and its wheels gripped the sand once more.

The 20-minute drive seemed to last for at least an hour. Perhaps unconsciously, everyone, including Woolf, breathed a sigh of relief when they finally, sharply, turned left and climbed a small dune that obscured a short drive-way beside a dark, two-story house that stood on structural stilts. It was one of several clusters of houses standing in alignment, directly facing the ocean, and all were on stilts as a precaution to the very real possibility of rising water.

As quickly as they could, they wrestled their luggage out of their respective vehicles and followed Robert up the steep steps and through the front door which he had unlocked. Once inside, he moved his hand along an inside wall, flipped on a light switch, and led them the rest of the way into the house. Kate and Zoe paused, temporarily blinded by the sudden, bright light. But, once their eyes had adjusted, they realized that they were facing a long room off to the right of the narrow, central hall, that was a combination dining and living room. A gas fireplace surrounded by two comfortable-looking armchairs and a couch, formed the center of the living-room area. This homey-looking space was separated from the dining area by a polished library table, the top of which was lined with assorted books and shells. A cathedral ceiling reached to the second floor, with a balcony that ran against the left wall. They could see closed doors set in the upstairs hall, and Kate wondered if those might be the bedrooms.

Robert allowed them only a moment to look around before he impatiently beckoned. "Come on, let's take this stuff upstairs."

"So, I was right about the bedrooms," Kate told herself. Her limited, prior experience of beach houses were those in which the bedrooms were on the lower floor, with the kitchen, living and dining spaces, located above.

She firmly gripped the handle of her suitcase as she and Zoe obediently followed Robert, whose typical arrogant attitude was a source of irritation to them both. Though Zoe was cautious about admitting this to Kate, Kate had no such scruples about frequently telling her mother what she thought of Robert. They had all just reached the upstairs hallway, when he stopped so abruptly that Kate bumped into her mother.

Robert, who seemed not to have noticed this, dropped his small suitcase in the middle of the hall and gestured impatiently toward the first door.

"Here, Zoe," he reached out, grasped her arm with one hand, and threw the door open with the other. "This is your room. It's the master bedroom and it also has the best view." He pointed at the two windows on the opposite wall. "See what I mean? You can look straight out onto the sea."

Without commenting, Zoe pushed past Robert and dropped her two suitcases next to the bed. "I'm not going to unpack anything just now," she said. Without pausing to either turn on a light or to look around, she followed him back out into the hall where Kate was leaning tiredly against the wall, and Woolf was patiently standing.

"Come on, Kate," Robert summoned her. "This is your room here, next to your mother's. And," he continued, "you also have a view of the sea. Or, at least you do from one of your windows. The other one gives you a glimpse, but is somewhat blocked by that big, scrub pine. But, one is better than none, don't you think?" He didn't wait for her to answer either way before he moved on to the other end of the hall.

Kate chose not to follow. Instead, she went into the room that Robert had assigned to her, and sat her suitcase and book-bag on the floor just inside the doorway. She yawned and stretched her arms over her head, then went to catch up.

"I'll take this back room..." Robert was saying, and then abruptly changed the subject. "Zoe, I probably should have mentioned this sooner, but I forgot about it. This other room," he nodded toward an additional closed door, "is kept locked, as you can see."

He looked thoughtful for a moment before explaining. "My friend who owns this house; his name is Graham, remember? He keeps some personal things in there. So, just leave that room alone. You've got plenty of space so it shouldn't be a problem, right?" He sniffed and slightly curled his lip as though daring either of them to argue the point.

Zoe, who recognized the unspoken challenge for what it was, was not intimidated. She merely raised her eyebrows and nodded toward the unusual combination lock on the outside of the door.

"Apparently, he *really* does want to make sure that no one peeks inside," she sarcastically observed. When Robert failed to answer, she shrugged her shoulders and added, "No, of course it's not a problem."

"Good." He looked at her appraisingly and nodded. "Then let's go back down and I'll show you the rest of the place."

Once downstairs again, he pointed out another room that was furnished as an office, and then led them to the back of the house where the kitchen and a small bathroom were located. Beyond the kitchen was a good-sized laundry room with a door that opened to the outside.

"Well, so that's everything," Robert declared as he pulled out a kitchen chair and dramatically threw himself into it. He heaved a sigh, snagged another chair with his foot, and pulled it closer. Then, he stretched out his long legs and propped both feet up on its seat.

"Bloody hell, but I'm tired," he moaned. Kate openly rolled her eyes at him, and mentally noted that this was now one of his favorite phrases, based on his groundless pretention to being British instead of American. He even managed to speak with an English accent at times, at least when he remembered to do so. Kate knew that Robert had seen her roll her eyes, but she couldn't have cared less. They stared at one another for a long moment before Robert looked away, and turned to her mother, instead.

"What happened to you, Zoe? I must have sat there for a half hour waiting for you!"

Zoe leaned back against the red-and-white countertop, stifled a yawn, and folded her arms.

"I'm sorry, Robert. Traffic was a lot worse than we had anticipated, and we spent a lot of time just trying to get through the Hampton Roads tunnel. I tried to call and tell you, but you didn't pick up."

He shook his head. "I must not have had a signal wherever I was at that time." Then he sighed again and stretched his arms up over his head while Kate's eyes narrowed. Zoe read her mind and shot her a quick, warning look as Robert sat up and spoke in a gentler tone.

"Zoe, are you and Kate going to be okay here? This is really a very lonely place and I may not have done you a favor by bringing you this far into the middle of nowhere."

"We'll be fine, Robert." She waved a dismissive hand in the air. "But, let's have some hot chocolate before we turn in. I could really use some, and I'm sure you could, too." She halted on her way to the refrigerator, turned, and looked intently at him. "There is some food here, right?"

"Yes," he reassured her. "It was delivered, as requested, and you can get whatever else you need tomorrow. There should be milk, chocolate and sugar, at the least."

A few minutes later, Zoe carefully poured the heated chocolate into tall, red, ceramic mugs that she'd found in one of the cupboards, passed them around, and sat down. Kate, who had been silently staring at the table, looked up and met her mother's eyes, and asked, "Will we be here for Thanksgiving?"

"No, Honey. We talked about this earlier, remember? We'll just be here for a couple of weeks."

Sensing that her daughter intended to pursue her quest to find out where they would actually spend the up-coming holiday, she carefully added, "We'll talk more about this tomorrow. And, meanwhile, Robert, we'll be fine. This is a great place to spend some time. Thanks for meeting us and bringing us all the way out here," she added, as she remembered her obligation to be polite.

"No problem, Zoe," he gestured at the room around them. "You know that I'd do anything for you and Kate." He impulsively reached across the table and laid his hand over Zoe's. Kate glared as she watched her mother gently pull her hand away and busily brush non-existent crumbs off the front of her sweater. A few moments of uncomfortable silence followed until finally, Robert stood up, stretched again, ran a hand through his long, unkempt hair, and spoke abruptly.

"Okay. Well, I'm off to bed and I'll leave first thing in the morning, probably before you're up." He turned to go, then added, "I'll check in with you every few days, and meanwhile, call or text me if you need anything. Oh, and I've left the house keys there, on the counter."

Robert pointed at the counter space next to the sink, but looked sideways toward Kate as though he couldn't help himself. She thrust her hands into her jeans pockets and stared back. Hiding her feelings had never been one of her strong points, especially where Robert was concerned. Consequently, he decided to punish her by not wishing her a good-night.

It was Zoe who stepped forward and broke the silence. "Sleep well," she smiled.

"Okay," he nodded, seemingly relieved, and added, "Good-night, all."

As Zoe took one last sip of her chocolate and headed for the sink, Kate whirled around to face her. "Mom..." her voice began to rise and Zoe quietly warned, "Not now. We'll talk tomorrow. In the morning. "

She sighed. "It will be fine, Kate; you'll see."

Kate reluctantly turned away then, and went up to her room. But later, when everyone seemed to be asleep, she found herself still staring at the white, ceiling fan that hung directly overhead. She slipped out of bed, and managed to avoid stepping on Woolf who was snugged down on the rug close-by. He opened his serious, dark eyes and watched her, though continued to lay still. She crossed over to her window and stood before the one that overlooked the sea.

Kate hesitated, not wanting to wake anyone, but then unlocked and raised it, and gasped as the cold, salty wind momentarily took her breath away. She could clearly hear the rough rhythm of the tide as it ebbed. She stood looking out, perhaps for only a few moments, when something below caught her eye. A whitish glow appeared near the edge of the shore, yet it didn't resemble any sort of light that she had ever seen before. It seemed to be moving and she thought that it must be someone taking a late-night stroll along the beach. Before she could make out what it was though, she saw the reflection of another light, that of a flashlight, moving close to their house. She pushed the window open wider, and heard their own front door open slowly, carefully, as though whoever it was, had no desire to draw attention to themselves.

Woolf heard it, too. He sat up and softly growled, but then the door closed as carefully as it had opened, and the light moved away. Kate tiptoed back across the room and opened her own door just a crack. She could see nothing, no light of any kind, but someone softly passed her door, and then she heard a door further up the hallway click softly shut. It must have been the door to Robert's room, she reasoned. She stood still for a little while and waited, but heard nothing more. Finally, Kate quietly closed her own door and moved back to the window to see if anything else could be seen. But, all was dark and quiet, so she climbed back into bed and Woolf resettled himself on the floor beside her.

Chapter Two

Early the next morning, Zoe, whose sleep had been unusually restless and laced with bad dreams, rose early. She pulled on a clean pair of jeans and a green, wool sweater that matched her eyes, though she had never noticed that it did. She absently brushed out her shoulder-length, red-gold hair in front of the mirror, but, her eyes and her mind were focused beyond the mirror and onto the deep-breathing sea outside her window. The grayish light before dawn vaguely illuminated the silver-surfaced water, but fog lay in heavy patches, obscuring any total view of the waking world without.

Knowing that Kate would very likely sleep for another couple of hours, Zoe carefully opened her daughter's bedroom door to let Woolf out and noticed that the door to Robert's room was wide-open.

"Good," she murmured to herself. "One less point of stress to deal with."

Moments later, she peered out the downstairs front window to double-check that Robert really had gone, and then passed through the kitchen to open the back door for Woolf, who went out and quickly returned. He was hungry, and she poured his food into a bowl, then measured coffee and water into the coffee-maker, for herself.

She searched the cupboards until she found a travel-mug with a lid, and, bending down, half-whispered, "You stay here, Woolf, and keep an eye on Kate for me, old boy." Her hand lingered on his silky head and she looked down into his fine, intelligent eyes and wondered, as she often had, what he was thinking. He always seemed to be so serious and thoughtful, and he clearly took his duty as their protector, very much to heart.

With a final pat, she rose and pulled on her fleece jacket, grabbed her scarf, and locked the door behind her. Except for the wind, it was dead silent outside. Even the gulls were quiet. As Zoe made her way toward the shore, an eerie sense of isolation enshrouded her, as did the clinging fog, which appeared to have thickened since she'd first observed it from her bedroom window.

Once she reached the water, she walked a good distance along the shore, away from the house. But, eventually, her movements grew more slow and hesitant as a heightened sense of uneasiness closed tightly around her. She tried to shake off the claustrophobic feeling, but still wondered in the back of her mind if she should have brought Woolf with her.

"Okay, enough is enough," she spoke aloud and consciously steadied herself. "I'm going back to the house and will take a walk later when this clears up." She abruptly turned around and shook her head at her own ability to scare herself. On the other hand, she really did have to admit that being isolated in the fog was spooky. But, surely the grayish shadows would lift with the sun. At the moment though, the sun was clearly losing the struggle, and for at least a little longer, the world would no-doubt remain suspended in twilight.

Zoe deeply breathed in the fresh, salt-air as she walked, and looked out at what could be seen, here and there, of the restless sea. She told herself that it wasn't only the fog that had urged her to turn around; she also intended to make a special breakfast for both Kate and herself on their first day at the Outer Banks. She needed to get started on that, she reasoned.

Quite suddenly, she noticed that the fog was transforming into a thick mist instead. As it lightened, she noticed a line of pelicans silhouetted against the lightening, gray sky, over the water. They were fishing for their breakfasts, dipping down, one after the other into the waves, then each rising once again, never breaking the evenness of their line as they continued to rise and fall. She stood and watched the birds for as long as she could see them, and then, unexpectedly, a stabbing realization of her own loneliness swept over her. It was strange how that feeling would creep up at times, usually when she least expected it.

"It's just the weather," she told herself. "The eeriness of the fog and now the mist." But, deep-down, she knew it was more.

"Alright," she admitted to herself, "so it's not just the weather." Along with that uncomfortable feeling was the knowledge that she and Kate really were alone now. She spoke aloud as though addressing an invisible presence hidden in the clouds. "And, what-on-earth am I going to do?"

There were times when the unanswered questions since her husband, David's, untimely death had come to feel almost like physical weight. She sometimes wondered if she and Kate would ever clearly find their way, again.

It seemed to her that her life had become a lot like that stubborn, early-morning fog she had wandered through. She simply couldn't see ahead well enough to make the best decisions for the future. In fact, she couldn't see more than a couple of steps ahead of herself. But, she reasoned, she and Kate had not been on their own for all that long either. After all, it wasn't quite a year, yet. Maybe things would just work out, though she admitted that currently, her hope seemed to be based on blind faith, alone. And, although she desperately loved her only child, she had come to realize that her bond with David had been the lifeline that had sustained them all. But, he was gone now. He had been a soldier, and he was dead. Killed in the line of duty in Iraq.

Secure in the knowledge that she was all alone on the shore, she looked out over the sea, and wistfully said, "David, we are so lost without you. What should we do, now?" Her words were caught and held for a moment by the wind before they dissolved.

She paused and looked out over the sea as though expecting some sort of sign. Then, with a sigh she turned to leave. But, instead, she stopped abruptly. A small, unexpected figure was emerging from out of the mist, and was striding purposefully towards her. As the figure came closer, she could see that it was a small, older woman with dark, and graying, hair.

The woman quickly strode up to her and firmly gripped her arm. Her expression was intense, but not unfriendly. However, Zoe, who was startled by the aggressive action from this strange little woman, instinctively tried to pull away and found that she couldn't. The woman's hand gripped her arm like a claw and she leaned in toward Zoe, nearly nose-to-nose, as she spoke. Her blue eyes earnestly searched Zoe's startled green ones.

"Did you see him, Dear?" she asked. Zoe, who had no idea what the woman was talking about, opened her mouth to protest, but the woman urgently interrupted her.

"I mean the horse. Last night. He is here again after all these years. Did you see him?"

Zoe still didn't understand, but somehow managed to pull her arm free and back up a few steps.

"No." She shook her head emphatically and looked indignant.

The woman, who appeared not to notice, took another step toward her and persisted. "Well, no doubt you will see him; usually people do, whenever he comes." She walked on, then turned back and shouted.

"He hasn't been here for many years, you know! I was just a little girl, then!"

Zoe made no attempt to answer, but turned instead and ran back toward the house as fast as the heavy sand would allow. It was with a great sense of relief that she reached the sandy grass that surrounded the house, and as she slowed her pace, she noticed that random rays of sunlight were finally piercing the gray ceiling of clouds. It was going to turn into a nice day, after all.

She unlocked the door, then quickly slammed and locked it behind herself, just in case the older woman might have decided to follow her. After all, she reasoned, the woman was clearly unbalanced and might be capable of who-knew-what. And as to the appearance of a horse, well, that should be nothing unusual. After all, wild horses had lived in this area for centuries. Zoe shivered as she hung up her jacket. Woolf, who had been asleep on the red and yellow rug in front of the stove, raised his head and gave her a questioning look.

Chapter Three

By the time Kate awoke, the sun had ascended into a clear, rich, blue sky such as one only sees in late autumn. The dark-gray clouds had been replaced by billowy, white ones that stretched across the horizon. It took a moment for her to remember where she was, and she happily drew in a deep breath. Then, she remembered, as she had every morning for the past 11 months. Her father was gone and would never come back to them—to her. She and her mother were told that he'd died honorably in active service in Iraq, but that meant very little to her, and she knew that it meant nothing more to her mother, either. What mattered, the only thing that mattered, was that he was not coming home again.

Kate sighed, rolled over, and noticed that Woolf was gone. Her mother had no doubt taken him outside since, according to the digital alarm clock beside her bed, it was already 9:00. She wondered if she should tell her mother about the front door opening and closing in the night, and then decided against it.

Robert had, perhaps, simply gone outside to retrieve something from his vehicle. And besides, her mother had enough on her mind to deal with; in fact, that was why they had come to the Outer Banks in the first place. Zoe and Kate were both struggling to adjust to life on their own, and Zoe was usually distracted and tired, in part from worrying about what they should do, and where they should live. Their coming here was Robert's idea; a way that work and rest might be combined and justified. Zoe had gathered photographs and was now finishing the text for a collections book, for the museum where she had worked as Curator of Collections for the past five years. Robert was the museum director.

He had arranged for them to stay at this house for a couple of weeks while her mother finished her work on the book. Kate had been removed from school, but she didn't care about that in the least. She would miss the couple of friends that she'd made, but certainly not the school where she was ridiculed for being a shy, quiet girl who preferred to read rather than talk very much. Some of her classmates had even given her a hard time because her father was a soldier. No, she wouldn't miss it. Secretly, she hoped that she would never have to go back there, and that her mother would just continue to home-school her as she planned to do while they stayed in this wonderfully isolated place.

Kate allowed herself the luxury of staying in bed a little longer, enjoying the idea of not having to get up to catch an early school bus. For a few moments, she pretended that this was their own house—her family's house— and that her dad was still alive, maybe downstairs joking with her mother and making a batch of his famous blueberry pancakes.

Kate heard Zoe downstairs, talking on the phone, from the sound of it, and then Woolf came in to check on her. He rested his chin on the edge of her bed and looked directly into her eyes, whimpered a little, and quietly uttered one, "Woof."

"Okay; I'm coming," she answered, and threw her legs over the side of the bed.

She pulled on a clean pair of jeans, a tee-shirt, and a sweater over that. Then, she washed her face, brushed her long, light-brown hair, and secured it with a stretchy, pink band. She wanted to re-explore the rest of the house, but decided that breakfast was, at this moment, a great deal more important. And, not too long afterward, she stood in the kitchen doorway, watching her mother who sat at the table, and who seemed to be deep in thought. Zoe held a cup of steaming, hot coffee in both hands and stared out of the window. In an attempt to appear as though she had not deliberately stood watching, Kate walked in, smothered a genuine yawn, and sat down in the chair opposite her mother's.

"Hey, Mom, is there anything decent to eat here?"

Startled, Zoe turned and looked at her. Her thoughts had been very far away, but she recovered quickly and answered with a gentle smile.

"Of course, Honey. Do you think I'd bring you out to this incredibly beautiful place and then not feed you?" Kate grinned back at her, and Zoe briskly rose from the table.

"What'll it be? Eggs or pancakes? We ought to celebrate our vacation here with a good breakfast on our first day." For a moment, Kate frowned as she thought of her dad's pancakes. But her expression cleared as she looked up at Zoe.

"Eggs," she said. "Definitely eggs this morning."

Chapter Four

"Who was that on the phone?" Kate asked as she finished the last of her creamy, scrambled eggs and buttered toast. She went to the sink and rinsed her plate and glass, and added them to the dishwasher. She was anxious to go outside, but instead, sat back down opposite her mother and waited for her answer.

"It was only Robert. He was checking on us and said to tell you 'Hello,' and that he hopes you like it here." Kate made a face and changed the subject.

"We were going to talk this morning, weren't we?" she persisted.

Zoe nodded, and an anxious expression clouded her eyes. "Yes, we are, and first of all, you know that we don't discuss our personal business in front of anyone, including Robert. Or, maybe I should say, especially in front of Robert." Kate nodded her agreement.

"Okay," Zoe continued, "so, we'll only be here for a couple of weeks, but we do need to talk about where we want to live, unless you want to stay where we are now, in Virginia. "

Kate leaned against the back of her chair until it rested on its two back legs, where she balanced by gripping the table's edge. "I thought we had to stay, because of your work."

"Put the chair down on the floor, Kate, before you fall," said her mother. "No, there is a possibility of finding other jobs in other places. But for now, your dad left us with enough money to be comfortable, even if I don't work for a while."

Kate leaned forward again and set the chair's legs firmly on the floor. She quietly absorbed her mother's words and added, "What about living near Aunt Susie in Connecticut? She says she wants us near her now."

Zoe's frown deepened. "Kate, you know that I love Aunt Susie. But, the problem is that she wants to take care of us. Absolute care of us. She means well, but she'll want to make our decisions. We are a family—you and me— and we need to make our own choices now that your dad is gone." She paused, and looked out of the window without really seeing beyond her own thoughts.

"No," she murmured a moment later. "it won't do at all. Susie will want to be in charge of our lives."

Kate impatiently brushed a strand of hair back from her face and asked, "Does Robert know?"

"Good heavens, no! Not yet, anyway," Zoe sighed. She spoke slowly and patiently. "I know you don't like him and that you're worried about his interest in me. But, Kate, I don't care for him so you don't need to worry about that. It's just that right now, I work for him and I need to get along with him."

Kate nodded her agreement without speaking, and her mother smiled. She had fully expected Kate to argue that she should not wait to leave her job and Robert. But, the truth was, Zoe felt that it wouldn't be right to begin a project, like this collections book, and then leave before it was finished.

This conversation with Kate had gone more easily than she had expected, and she was relieved. Kate could be stubborn, she thought, and then reminded herself that her daughter might well have inherited that trait from herself.

"Any other questions?" she asked.

In answer, Kate stood up and reached out to hug her mother, but Zoe pulled the girl down onto her lap instead, and wrapped her arms tightly around her daughter. Kate rested her head on her mother's shoulder and, in a small, quiet voice, said, "I've just been so scared that you might marry Robert."

"Oh, Sweetheart. There is no way that I would marry anyone that you don't like. Also, we just lost your dad a year ago, and I don't want to think about anyone else, yet. Maybe never. And believe me," she emphatically added, "I would never consider Robert as a possible candidate!"

Kate grinned and Zoe gently patted her back. Neither of them spoke for a few minutes, and Zoe assumed that Kate was mulling over some other unasked questions. But, Kate said nothing more, and her mother anxiously asked, "Are you okay, now?"

"Absolutely," said Kate, and hugged her mother even tighter. Unexpected tears of relief welled up in her brown eyes, but she blinked them away before letting her mother see her face, again.

"Can we stay here if we want to?" she sniffed into Zoe's shoulder.

"Well, let's wait and see if we *do* want to," Zoe answered. "We could probably rent another house out here, but I have decided that when our two weeks in this house ends, I'll turn in my resignation, whatever we decide to do. I'll have the collections book finished by that time, and you know that's the only reason that I am still working for Robert. Just to honor that commitment."

A comfortable silence settled over them both, and Kate gave her mother an additional quick, hard hug and then got up off her lap. "Okay, I'm going outside now."

Zoe got up too, and pushed in her chair. "Wait a minute; watch out for the cars and trucks on this beach, and don't go too far from the house. Oh! And, did I tell you that there are wild horses out here?"

Kate's eyes grew large. "No, you didn't! Why are they here? How many are there?"

Zoe smiled again, this time at the surprised look on her daughter's face.

"They are one of the last wild herds in this country, and they descend from the mustangs that were brought here by the Spanish in the 1500s. I've read that when ships would get caught up on the sand bars in shallow water and wreck, the horses on board were usually able to swim ashore. Other times, when the ships were simply stuck, the crew would get rid of any additional weight so that they could float again. In which case, the horses were set free."

"The thing is," Zoe grew serious, "they are wild. And, they're protected, and they can be dangerous. So, if you see any horses on the beach or on the dunes around us, admire them from afar. And, by all means let me know, because I'm dying to see them, too!

"Wow, okay—I'll do that," answered Kate, and then hesitated. "But what about Woolf?"

Zoe glanced down at the black-and-tan German shepherd who lay quietly beside the door, and shook her head.

"Woolf won't bother them; don't worry about it. You know he won't leave your side unless he's protecting you. Just don't walk toward the horses if you see them, and he will stay with you."

Zoe pushed back her hair, walked to the window, and changed the subject.

"I can't get over how different the light looks here. By the way, we're going to do some shopping this afternoon, after lunch. For now though, off you go. Zip up your jacket—it may look warmer outside than it really is. I was out early this morning and it was pretty chilly then." She said nothing about the eerie fog, nor did she mention the strange, old woman whom she had encountered.

As Kate and Woolf went out, Zoe finished loading the dishwasher and reluctantly trod back up the hall to the office. She would so much rather have gone out with Kate and Woolf, but did need to finish the book. And so, with a sigh, she reluctantly made herself sit down and turn on the computer. And, sincerely hoped that the internet service wasn't going to slow her down.

Chapter Five

Kate and Woolf scrambled over the small dune in front of their house, careful to avoid the clumps of swaying sea-oats that clung to the sand. They pushed ahead to the bit of shoreline opposite their house. Kate looked around, and saw that, at least for the time being, all was quiet. There were no cars or trucks, and no horses either. So, she and Woolf walked back and forth, scanning the beach for small treasures that the tide might have washed up. They didn't go far, though there were miles of open shoreline in either direction, as far as they could see.

The wind blew, as it always does near the sea. But, the air was mildly warm, in spite of the season being late fall. When she tired of walking, Kate sat down on the sand near the water's edge, idly sifted it with her fingers, and watched the sea birds glide and dip through the waves, intent on their fishing. She reflected that flying must feel like surfing on air.

As always though, her thoughts eventually turned to her dad. Before he had left them for the last time, he had said that when he came back, he would teach her how to surf. As Kate watched the outgoing tide, her mind returned to the present moment and she suddenly noticed clear, deep, hoof prints in the sand in front of her. A horse had obviously stood there, but since then, the waves had to have covered those prints. So, why were they still sharp and clear-looking? They should have shifted and faded with the tide.

Before she could think any further about it though, she was distracted by Woolf, who uttered a faint growl from deep in his throat. His ears had perked up and he was watching something. She shaded her eyes, hoping to see horses, but instead saw a young girl, small and thin, with long, black hair. The girl was standing very still and was staring at the two of them. She looked as though she might want to approach them, but instead, kept her distance and stood quietly, some 20 feet away, at the edge of the shore.

Kate raised her hand and waved, and the girl waved back. Woolf closely watched, but had ceased to growl. Finally, Kate called out, "Hi! Do you live around here?"

Perhaps the girl couldn't hear Kate's words above the sound of the waves, because she didn't answer. After a moment's hesitation, Kate got up, dusted the sand off her jeans, and walked, closely accompanied by Woolf, to where the girl waited. The expression on the younger girl's face was both eager and anxious. She was also very pale and her dark-brown eyes were solemn. She nervously clasped her hands together and waited. Kate first wondered if the girl had really just wanted to be left alone, but then she considered the possibility that perhaps she was shy. Well, thought Kate, it was too late now. So, she took the initiative and introduced herself.

"My name is Kate and this is Woolf," she nodded and gestured proudly toward her dog. But suddenly she, herself, felt shy, and so she leaned over, put her arm around Woolf's neck and laid her head on top of his. Her hair, pulled loose from the pink band, fell forward and hid her face, and partially hid his, as well.

If Kate expected the girl to introduce herself though, she was surprised. The girl said nothing about herself, and only asked, "Will he hurt me?" She stood very still, as though afraid to move.

"No!" Kate snapped, outraged on Woolf's behalf. She was surprised and indignant at the idea that anyone would doubt Woolf's character, including this scared-rabbit-looking girl.

"Please don't be mad," the girl pleaded, and took a step closer. "It's just that I've never been around animals much because my dad doesn't like them."

Kate couldn't help but wonder if Sarah's dad was as unappealing as Robert was, because he didn't like animals, either. He only thought of them as dirty, and possibly disease-ridden, nuisances. Good reasons, as far as he was concerned, to keep them at a distance from himself. Unfortunately though, Kate reflected, Woolf's presence didn't seem to keep him away from either her mother, or their home.

"That's okay then," she answered stiffly. "Woolf is my best friend though, and he wouldn't hurt anyone unless they were trying to hurt me or my mom."

"You're really lucky," said the girl, her large eyes looking even more solemn than before. "Would it be okay if I petted him?" She took another step, closer. "I'm Sarah, and I was just wondering if you've moved here."

Kate looked down at Woolf. "Sure; he won't mind." She unnecessarily added, "Just be gentle with him." Then, she answered, "We're only here for a couple of weeks while my mom finishes a book for work. She's a museum curator."

Her words brought an unexpected smile to Sarah's thin face, though the girl continued to nervously twist her hands together and she dropped her eyes while she prodded the wet sand with the toe of her stained, sodden sneaker.

"Maybe we could be friends while you're here?" Her solemn expression was momentarily replaced by a hopeful one.

Kate grinned back at her, feeling as though a temporary friendship might be possible, as long as Woolf's character and presence were not in question. Besides, having someone nearby who was close to her own age might be fun.

"Yes. I'd like that," she answered.

They shyly eyed each other for a moment and then Kate asked, "Do you want to come back with me to my house? You could stay and eat lunch with us. I mean, you could ask your mom if it's okay, first."

"It's just me and my dad; my step-dad actually," Sarah shrugged. "And he's gone for the day, so it'll be okay."

"Great. I think we're having grilled cheese sandwiches."

As the girls slowly strolled back to the house together, Kate looked sideways at Sarah and asked, "Aren't you in school?"

"No," she emphatically shook her head. "Dad pays someone to home-school me, but she only comes a couple of days each week, and I've caught up with all of my assignments. They're pretty boring most of the time, though I do like to read when I can read what I want."

"Me, too!" Kate grinned again.

"I saw you from our front window and wanted to meet you," Sarah said. "That's why I came out to the shore. It's really lonely here sometimes," she added.

The girls entered the house through the back laundry room. They paused to hang up their jackets and then Kate led Sarah through to where Zoe sat at a heavy, oak desk and staring at her computer screen.

"Hi, Mom," Kate called. "I've met a new friend and her name is Sarah."

Zoe swung around in her chair, relieved at the interruption.

"Hi, Sarah," she sounded pleased. But, before she could say anything more, Kate quickly said, "We're going up to my room. Let us know when lunch is ready, okay?" And, the girls disappeared upstairs.

Zoe found herself humming a tune she hadn't thought of in years. She was pleased that Kate had found a new friend. The girl needed someone her own age to spend time with. With a pang, Zoe reflected that it had been a long time since she had seen Kate excited about anything or had heard her genuinely laugh. That just isn't right, she reflected. David had been dead for nearly a year; it was time to live again, and to move on. For both of them.

An hour or so later, as Zoe pulled out a skillet large enough to accommodate three grilled cheese sandwiches, she realized that she, herself, also needed someone to laugh with, and to spend time with, again. Well, that would come. The main thing, she told herself, was that Kate should find those things, first. Kate's happiness and well-being mattered more than anything else.

Sarah was smaller than Kate, but was probably about the same age, she guessed.

Not long after, when they all sat down to eat together, Sarah's shyness quickly evaporated. Among other things, she told them that she was also 11-years- old, and reiterated that her dad was really her step-dad. Zoe noted that she said nothing about either her mother or her real dad, and she wondered.

Chapter Six

As they zipped up their jackets and prepared to leave, Kate asked, "What about Woolf, Mom?"

Zoe considered what might be best, and made her decision. "Woolf won't come with us this time. We'd probably have to leave him in the Jeep, and I don't want him to have to wait too long for us."

She bent over and stroked the warm head that stood close beside her, wordlessly apologizing to him for leaving him behind. He looked up, expectantly, but she said, "No, Woolf; not this time. You stay here and guard the place for us." He whimpered, but obediently sat and watched as Zoe locked the door behind them, and left him there alone.

Sarah had been invited to come along, and she eagerly climbed into the sun-warmed, back seat with Kate. Zoe drove slowly back, the way they had come the night before. They had not gone very far before they saw two horses standing near the shore. One was black and the other, a chestnut.

"Oh, Mom! Look!" Kate cried, half hanging out her open window and pointing. Zoe parked the Jeep a distance away from the horses, and they all got out.

"Remember, Kate," her mother warned, "you have to stay at least 50 feet away from them."

"But why, Mom?" Kate pleaded. "Why can't we walk up to them? They look friendly."

Kate's voice rose along with her frustration, in spite of what her mother had told her about the horses earlier, and she impatiently stamped her foot. "Look; that one is watching us. I wish I had something to give them to eat."

"No, Kate, you can't do that," Zoe insisted. "But, I'll tell you what we *will* do; we'll stop at the *Corolla Wild Horse Fund* while we're in Corolla. They will explain why we should neither approach, nor feed, the horses. Believe it or not, these rules are for everyone's good."

They climbed back into the Jeep, and Kate slumped back into her seat, convinced that her mother was over-reacting. But, she didn't say anything more. After all, there was no point since Zoe obviously wasn't open to negotiations. As Sarah settled in beside her, she leaned over and whispered.

"She's right, Kate. I've lived here as long as I can remember, and those horses can hurt you, and you can make them sick by feeding them stuff. You'll see," she confidently added.

Kate just shrugged and looked out the window. Her mother had mentioned the 50-foot law earlier, but now that she'd actually seen them, she had found it hard to obey.

Not too long afterward, they slowly and carefully climbed the sand-hill back onto the main road, and within minutes, turned onto another road that led into the parking lot near the old, red-brick, Currituck Lighthouse.

"I wanted to show you this first, Kate; isn't it great?" Zoe asked.

Kate, who was still irritated with her mother, didn't bother to answer. Meanwhile, Zoe parked the Jeep, and they all got out and walked over to see it up close. Standing in the brown-green grass, fairly close to one other, were three buildings—the Lighthouse, an old, double-house situated directly across from its entrance, and another small, white house extravagantly trimmed with Victorian gingerbread work, that currently housed a gift-shop. A thick forest of trees and undergrowth covered the land between the main road and the cluster of buildings.

In spite of herself, Kate abandoned her earlier frustration and silence. "Wow, Mom! Do they still use this lighthouse?" Her eyes widened with excitement.

"Absolutely, Honey," Zoe grinned. "I've been reading about it. But, the Coast Guard keeps the Lighthouse, now. It was built in the 1870s, I believe, and over there," she pointed, "that double-house, is where the two keepers once lived. And, see that pretty little house with the *Lighthouse Museum Shop* sign? A third lighthouse keeper lived there, once upon a time."

They looked over the buildings and visited the gift-shop, then walked the short distance that led to the rest of the village. It was a very small, but charming village. The few old houses they passed were set within, what would be during the summer, deeply-shaded lawns. And, there was a one-room schoolhouse—still in use—which Kate marveled at. Not far from the schoolhouse, was the *Corolla Wild Horse Fund and Museum*, where they found a good assortment of horse-related merchandise and a couple of friendly volunteer employees.

As they chatted, Kate was silently grateful that her mom didn't make a big fuss in front of them, about how she had wanted to break their rules and pet and feed the wild horses they'd seen on the beach. Instead, Zoe asked questions as though she, herself, wanted clarification about the rules.

"Are the horses dangerous; is that why we aren't allowed to go within 50 feet of them?" Zoe asked a lovely, young woman, with shining, brown eyes, who had introduced herself to them as Mandy.

Mandy tossed back her long, honey-brown hair and nodded. "Yes. They are wild, and they can easily hurt or even kill a person. But also, that is a law. And, we do want them to remain wild by not having contact with humans. If they interact with people, they have to leave the herd because they will endanger themselves and the rest of the herd, too. The bottom-line is that these are *wild* horses, and they need to remain wild."

"And why can't people feed them? Wouldn't that actually help out?"

"Absolutely not," Mandy emphatically shook her head. "They eat a special, balanced diet, and other types of food can cause colic, which makes them very sick and can even kill them. We make these rules to protect the horses as well as the people who come to see them. We want you to enjoy seeing them in their natural, wild state, but these laws are enforced for everyone's well-being. "

She went on to tell them that though she volunteered in the Museum sometimes, she also had a lot of medical knowledge and experience working directly with the herd. The girls were thrilled, and Kate thought that when she grew up, she wanted to be just like Mandy.

Zoe changed the subject then, and asked what else was around, and whether or not there was a village grocery store. As they left, the girls waved good-bye, and Mandy told them to come and see her again, anytime. Kate mentally made a note to do just that. She really wanted to come again, and was sure that her mother would bring her back. She wanted to know more about the horses.

Chapter Seven

The sun was shining as they crossed the street behind the *Corolla Wild Horse* building, and walked over to where two inviting, white rockers stood side-by-side on the wide, front porch of the *The Old Village Store.* The building was covered with weathered, silver shingles and was flanked on either side by large, oak trees. Rose bushes grew beside each of the white-painted railings, and, remarkably, a few, late, red roses still bloomed.

Sarah, who was pleased to be showing her new friends around, led the way into the store where a stout woman, perhaps in her 60s, sat in a comfortable arm-chair near the door. A ready smile was on her face as soon as she heard the door open, and she leisurely pushed her glasses back up on her nose, got up, and took her position behind the counter.

"Hi, Sarah," she called out. "Are you going to introduce me to your friends?"

Sarah's dark eyes shone. "Hi, Mrs. Hoskins," she smiled, and tugged at her own hair. "This is Kate and her mother. They're renting the Owens house, close to ours. But, only for a couple of weeks."

Mrs. Hoskins welcomed them, her friendly grin never wavering. "Glad to have you folks here. It's not the best time of the year, but maybe you'll come back again in the spring. Now," she said briskly,

"What can I help you find?"

Zoe set about collecting more essentials such as additional milk, bread, cereal, and butter, and then moved on to the non-essentials that included ingredients to bake with. She had promised the girls chocolate-chip cookies for dessert. Meanwhile, Sarah and Kate looked around, half listening to the non-stop conversation between the adults. Mrs. Hoskins had long-since insisted that Zoe call her by her first name, which was Rose. At first, Kate was distracted by the things in the shop, but, once she had tuned back in to the women's conversation, she heard the word, "haunted."

"Yes, Ma'am; that's exactly right," Rose emphatically slapped a hand on the counter in front of her, causing specks of fine dust to rise into the air. "There's some who have seen some things they shouldn't have, and at that house where you're staying, too. Lights flashing on and off when nobody is there. And then, there are the stories about other Outer Banks ghosts, of course."

She broke off abruptly as the screen door creaked open and slammed shut, and suddenly a tall, well-built man with dark-blond hair and brilliant blue eyes was standing next to Zoe at the counter. He looked as though he might be in his 40s, and he wore a Currituck County deputy's uniform.

Rose grinned at him, resumed her ghostly narrative long enough to finish what she'd been saying, and then asked, "Isn't that right, Hugh? You've heard those stories too, haven't you?"

The man threw his head back and chuckled. "What-on-earth are you telling these folks, Rose? Are you trying to scare them into leaving sooner than they'd planned?"

He turned to Zoe and directly met her eyes. "You *are* visitors here, aren't you? I don't believe I've seen you around here before."

Without waiting for an answer, the deputy introduced himself as Hugh McKenzie. He shook hands with them both, and then ruffled Sarah's hair because he knew very well who she was, and she obviously liked him. Her eyes shone even brighter as he bent over to look directly into her face.

"How are you, Miss Sarah, and where is your dad off to, today?" His warm, teasing smile was infectious, and Sarah, a wide, answering grin on her own, thin face, blossomed at his attention to her.

She shrugged her shoulders and beamed. "I don't know. He just said that he had to pick up some stuff and deliver it to somebody by this afternoon. He said he'd be gone late...but I'm going to eat dinner with Zoe and Kate tonight, and maybe spend the night, too! We're going to make chocolate chip cookies!"

Hugh rested his hands on his thighs and answered. "That sounds mighty good, Miss Sarah. If I stop by later, can I have one of those cookies?"

He looked up and winked at Zoe, and though she felt obliged to invite him because he had just invited himself, she was startled. She let it pass, though. After all, he was a deputy. Besides which, she and Kate were currently staying in a very isolated area, and maybe it wouldn't hurt to be on friendly terms with him.

As she gathered up her grocery bags, Hugh added, "Hey, how about you girls having some lunch with me at *Aunt Susie's Place*, over there? They've got the best, darned, charcoal-grilled hamburgers and chicken barbeque that you'll find anywhere. Biscuits, too. And, if you ever come by for breakfast, be sure and try their sausage biscuits. Everyone who comes to Corolla has to eat there, at least once," he joked.

Rose pushed her glasses up farther on her nose as she chuckled and nodded in agreement, while Zoe explained that they'd already had lunch. But, he insisted that they at least walk over with him and get something to take home for their dinner.

"After all, you'll be so busy making those cookies that you won't want to cook dinner, too," he rationalized, as he pushed his hat to the back of his head and then pulled it forward again.

"Tell you what; I'll buy. That'll be my thanks for sharing those cookies later, and then you can consider yourselves to be officially welcomed here."

He seemed really pleased with himself, which further fueled Zoe's growing irritation at the deputy's aggressive friendliness. But, she couldn't think of a polite reply quickly enough.

"He's a run-away-train," she thought. "Maybe we *won't* stay here as long as we'd planned."

His attitude reminded her of the not-infrequent encounters she had with other aggressive and competitive people, including Robert, whose moods were mercurial, to say the least. She had no intention of putting up with such people on her own time, though.

However, seemingly confident and blissfully unaware of the bad impression he had made, Hugh waved them over to an outdoor table, one of several, while he went inside and ordered their food.
"We could eat inside, but it's such a pretty day I thought you folks might like to sit out here instead," he
said. "Even if you're taking your food home with you, it's just a nice place to sit for a little while."

To Kate's delight, just as they were pulling out their chairs, two plump, and very vocal, hens rushed across the quiet street to join them.

"Hey, I see you've met Lucy and Ethel," Hugh laughed, as he carried the food over to where they sat. "These girls love the biscuits here, so we'll have to share some of it with them. I never have the heart to hurt their feelings, even if they are chickens. See," he broadly gestured, "when you eat here, you never eat alone. As long as you eat outside, that is," he grinned.

Soon after, Zoe and the girls, minus some of their biscuits, closed the lids on their Styrofoam boxes of food and abruptly left Hugh seated at the table eating his lunch, closely accompanied by the two companionable hens who weren't about to pass up their chance for even more food.

"Okay," announced Zoe as she smoothed down her jacket and headed for the Jeep, "let's go bake some cookies."

Chapter Eight

A couple of hours later, the smell of warm, chocolate-chip cookies filled the house. While they cooled, Zoe presided over a sink full of soapy dishwater as the girls, dishtowels in hand, dried and put everything away.

For a shy girl, Sarah had quickly turned talkative, and filled them in on the rest of their neighbors. She also mentioned that she was left alone much of the time, sometimes even at night. She confided that there had been a couple of times when she'd been scared and had hidden in the back of her closet behind her clothes.

Zoe asked what her step-father did, and she explained that he was often hired to pick up freight, usually brought in on small fishing boats, which he would then deliver to his customers by either using his own boat or his cargo-van. He had a couple of business partners, but Sarah had never met them, and had no idea what sort of freight he dealt with.

To herself, Zoe questioned the fact that Sarah was left alone a lot, but then reasoned that close neighbors in this isolated place might well take care of each other, which brought her back to thinking about Hugh.

She had no doubt that Hugh would show up this afternoon, especially as he had invited himself. She considered asking him about Sarah's home-situation, but then quickly decided against it. For all she knew, he might be good friends with Sarah's step-father and maybe even a business partner, too. She wondered if Robert knew the man. Maybe she would ask him when they spoke again, just to see what he might say.

The afternoon passed quickly, and as the sun descended into the darkening horizon, the doorbell rang. Sure enough, it was Hugh, wearing the same wide grin on his face.

"Hey, there," his voice rang out. "Am I too early to beg some cookies from you?"

Zoe, with a watchful Woolf at her side, consciously composed her face into what she hoped was a welcoming expression, and then stepped aside, holding the door for him. "Sure; come on in."

Before she could lead the way to the warm kitchen though, he surprised her further. "Say, is there, by chance, anything that I can help you with around here? I'm a pretty handy guy and I'd like to earn my chocolate chip cookies."

Zoe's carefully conceived, welcoming expression, slipped into non-existence and she abruptly answered. "No—thank you. We just arrived here last night," she gestured at the open room, "and everything is undoubtedly fine."

Hugh's smile faded just as quickly, and he defensively held up his hands.

"Okay, I'm sorry. I didn't mean to offend you." His tone grew quieter and more serious. "It's just that you're out here on your own and if there's anything that needs fixing, I can probably help you with it rather than your having to wait for somebody to come out and take care of it."

His shrewd eyes directly met her stern ones, and neither spoke. Then, he removed his hat, cleared his throat, looked up at the ceiling, and then back at her, again.

"I live just three houses away from you." He vaguely waved his hand in the direction of his house. "If anything is a problem, or even if you're ever just scared for some reason, I'll be glad to help you out. Not that you don't have good protection here," he diplomatically added, his eyes focused on Woolf who stood beside her.

"Look," he reached into his pocket and pulled out a business card. "Here, take this. I've written my cell phone number on the back. Okay? Just in case?"

Zoe audibly sighed as she reached out and accepted the card. She stuffed it into her shirt pocket, and silently waved him back into the kitchen. Without another word, she pulled out a chair for him at the table where the girls sat, waiting. In the middle of the table rested a large plate of cookies. Each of the girls had a glass of milk, but Hugh opted for hot tea, so she prepared a pot for them to share.

As they talked, Hugh managed to keep the conversation casual and pleasant, though Zoe watched him closely and noted that he did, thankfully, either consciously or otherwise, drop his hearty persona. While she acknowledged that she probably couldn't have stood much more of his former pushiness, she was equally suspicious about the change in him.

He chiefly chatted with the girls, and it wasn't long before Kate managed to bring up the subject of ghosts, again. Zoe figured that sooner or later she would, and inwardly groaned. She hadn't much patience with anything supernatural; what really mattered, in her view, was the here-and-now. Hugh glanced at her as though expecting exactly that reaction from her, then turned his attention back to what Kate was saying. Meanwhile, Zoe fervently hoped that Kate's sudden interest in ghosts wasn't rooted in the hope of seeing her dead father, again.

Finally, as Hugh swallowed the remainder of his sixth cookie and reached for the seventh, he spoke, but, not about ghosts. "Wow, these are really good. I've eaten more of them than I meant to," and he pulled his hand away from the plate, instead.

"No, please," said Zoe, who had finally begun to feel a little more kindly toward him. "Take as many as you want; we have enough ingredients to make another batch and the girls would enjoy doing that tomorrow. Right, Girls?"

She glanced at the clock and said to Sarah, "You're welcome to spend the night with us and help make more cookies, but you had better ask your dad if that's okay, and let him know where you are, too. "

Sarah's face lit up. "I'm sure it will be okay with him!" she bubbled.

"Okay. Well, the phone is over there next to the door; go and call him right now."

While Sarah was busy doing that, Hugh thoughtfully chewed his cookie and looked at Kate. "The Outer Banks has a lot of ghost stories; in fact, you'll see a lot of books about them in the shops. For tourists mostly. You see, a lot of stories are told amongst the locals that never go into the books."

He paused as though lost in his own thoughts before adding, "I could tell you at least one of them, Kate, but only if it's okay with your mom. What do you think, Zoe?"

She drew a deep breath, considered her answer carefully, and then agreed. The girls would undoubtedly enjoy it, and she was probably making too much of Kate's sudden interest in ghosts. After all, most kids liked spooky stories, and Halloween was less than a week away. It was probably just a natural kid-thing.

At that moment, Sarah hung up the phone, pleased that her dad had said she could spend the night. Kate had already headed upstairs to fetch the book of Virginia ghost stories that she'd found in her room. Sarah, seeing that Kate had gone, literally skipped down the hall and ran up the steps to find her and tell her the good news about staying over.

Zoe and Hugh were left together, sitting in a semi-comfortable silence, as they waited for the girls to return. That is, until Zoe leaned back in her chair, folded her arms, and sweetly asked, "Tell me, Deputy McKenzie, are you always this friendly to Outer Banks visitors?" Her smile took some of the sting away from her words, though he clearly understood that she suspected an ulterior motive in his friendliness.

Hugh hadn't expected that, and instinctively looked away while he carefully considered his answer. In the end, he decided that the truth was probably best. "Okay," he admitted, looking down at the table. He absent-mindedly picked up a cookie-crumb and dropped it into his napkin before continuing.

"I guess I'm not too good at this," he said. But, when he looked up again, he was relieved to see amusement in her eyes instead of anger.

"I mean, I'm not good at pretending; not at being a deputy. I'm actually a pretty good deputy," he quietly added.

Zoe's laugh rang out. His expression was that of a guilty, little boy who had been caught doing something he shouldn't. But, unaware of this, his thoughts were elsewhere. He had suddenly realized that he liked this woman. She was smart and definitely no push-over. Maybe she was no game-player either; he hoped not because it would make everything easier. He unconsciously nodded as he acknowledged his growing respect for her.

"How well do you know Graham Owens who owns this house?" he abruptly asked.

"I don't know him at all," she shot back. "I've neither met him nor spoken with him. I rented this place through a friend of his, Robert Caldwell."

"I work for Robert," she explained. " I'm just here for a couple of weeks to finish a book and," she hesitantly added, "to get away for a little while, though perhaps that's not going to happen now for some reason that you know of?" Her eyebrows rose.

"Let me explain," he said, closely watching her reactions. "I am convinced that something is going on at this house. We've been watching it for the past six months or so. Way-too-many people are coming and going from here, especially at night. And, by the way, I really do live only three houses down from here, and I've seen a lot of activity at times—people coming and going, I mean."

"You know," he continued, "in an isolated place like this, people could be smuggling drugs, or who-knows-what. A place like this is wonderful; it's so wild and free. But, it's also an easy haven for those who intend to break the law."

Zoe sighed. "So, I guess that you're officially interrogating me, right?"

Hugh threw back his head and laughed. "Not really. I don't really believe that you have anything to do with what's been happening here, but I was hoping that you might be able to help shed some light on it."

He abruptly added, "Would you mind taking me on a tour of the house, since I'm already here?"

"Sure," she stood up. "On the other hand, I can't imagine that it's going to be much help to you."

"I would truly appreciate it, whether anything turns up or not," he hastily answered, relieved that she wasn't angry and was willing to cooperate.

Together, they walked upstairs and Zoe first showed him their bedrooms, then paused in front of the locked door. "Robert said that the owner keeps his own things locked away in here, which seems perfectly natural, to tell you the truth, although, that is *quite* an unusual lock, don't you think?"

Hugh whistled softly. "I agree, but that combination lock would be the best type to keep anyone out. I could easily jimmy a regular one and make it look like I hadn't, but this is another story. So, I guess for now, we'll just have to leave it."

The girls, still chatting animatedly with each other, came out of Kate's room and followed them downstairs to tour the rooms on the lower floor. Not wanting to either frighten the girls or raise their suspicions, Hugh grinned at them and said, "Hey, I've always wanted to see what the inside of this house looks like. I'm thinking of doing some remodeling on my place and I need ideas."

Kate, whose mind was on the evening ahead, anxiously asked, "Are you still going to stay and tell us ghost stories, Mr. McKenzie? I'd really like to hear them and Sarah would, too."

Sarah looked less enthusiastic about the stories than Kate did, but was obviously unwilling to say anything that might disagree with the desires of her new friend.

Hugh paused and turned to Zoe, who stood behind him. "What do you think?"

"I think it would be fun. Kate enjoys a good, spooky story, and Sarah seems okay with the idea, as well. But first, I'm going to make some dinner for us, so have a seat but don't get too comfortable because it will be ready before long.

"What about the chicken barbeque," he asked.

"Men, nor women for that matter, can live on barbeque alone, Deputy McKenzie. I was saving it for tomorrow's lunch," she explained.

A short time later, they all sat down to a dinner that included roast chicken, tossed salad, and homemade cornbread. Periods of silence interspersed their friendly conversation, because they were all very hungry. Finally, when everyone had finished, Zoe stood up and began to collect the plates and silverware. Hugh quickly jumped up, as well.

"Let me help you," he said. "Believe me, I've enjoyed eating a meal that I didn't have to cook, for a change. It was all really great."

Once everything was rinsed and loaded into the dishwasher, Zoe shooed them from the room. "Go on into the living room; I'm going to make some popcorn while you all get comfortable, and I'll only be a few minutes."

"Mind if I light up that gas fireplace?" Hugh asked. "A good fire will drive out the chill and make the night cozier."

Zoe nodded her agreement. "That's a great idea; go right ahead."

Chapter Nine

Night had fallen and pale wisps of clouds floated across a thin, crescent moon by the time everyone was settled together in the living room. The girls sat propped up against pillows on either end of the comfortable red-plaid couch, their legs stretched out so that their toes almost touched. They shared a crocheted, white afghan, and they each had cups of hot cocoa and bowls of popcorn perched on the end tables that stood on either side of the couch.

Zoe leaned back in an oak, rocking chair that was positioned close beside the hearth where the gas fire blazed. She was sleepy, more tired than she'd realized, and hoped that the caffeine in the cocoa was enough to keep her awake a little while longer. Her hair was tousled and her pale, make-up-free face looked younger than her 38 years. Hugh sat in a plush, chintz armchair across from her, and gazed with unseeing eyes into the heart of the otherwise darkened room. His sight was inward, focused on other places and times. Finally, he broke the silence.

"Ghost stories about the Outer Banks mostly focus on pirates, possible hidden treasure, deliberately-wrecked ships and dead men who don't talk. Women, too. Women who trusted the wrong men, and some women who were pirates, too, believe it or not. These are the kinds of stories that you'll find in the books. But, I want to tell you a local story that you won't find written down. At least, as far as I know."

The girls leaned forward, toward him, as though on cue.

"You've seen some of the wild horses here, right?" They all nodded.

"The herd only includes about 100 horses these days, and these mustangs are black or brown; darker or lighter shades of such. But, in the old days, a white horse would be born into the herd once in a while, too. It was rare, and people were superstitious about them. Many thought that the white horses had special powers and brought good luck; I guess because they *were* so rare. No white horses have been seen for a long time now, even the one known hereabouts as the Ghost Horse."

"Stories about this horse date back quite a ways, but, as far as I know, the last time he was seen was during the 1920s, though one of my neighbors claims she saw him when she was a little girl, back in the 50s. He's a little larger than most of the horses out here. You know, mustangs are small as far as horses go, but they're tough and hearty, and strong. They're smart, too. And they're survivors. Obviously. Otherwise, they'd have never lasted here on their own for the last 400 years."

"Anyway, folks who've seen this horse, say that he only appears rarely, and only when someone is facing great trouble. He doesn't just come as a warning, though; help seems to follow him. I'm going to tell you one of the stories that was told to me by an old fisherman who lived on this wild coast all of his life. He's dead now, and even though I really don't believe in ghosts, nor have I ever seen this horse, still, I believe this man's story."

Hugh sipped his cocoa and cleared his throat, then took in a deep breath and slowly released it. "Okay, ladies; I don't claim to be a good story-teller, but, here it is."

The fisherman's name was Jack, and like I said, he lived here all of his life. His dad was a fisherman too, and it was a hard life. For that matter, it's still a hard life, but it was a lot tougher in those days. Jack's mother and young brother, Eli, helped with the fishing and kept everything going, through the good times and the bad. And, there were plenty of both.

Back in the early 20s, Jack's dad suddenly got really sick and died. They never did find out what was wrong with him, but he went fast, and then there they were, on their own. Jack was only 13 years old at the time, but he tried to take his dad's place and to do enough fishing to keep the family together. The alternative would have meant that they would have been separated, split up, and sent to wherever people who were too poor to survive on their own, had to live.

Jack said his mother was near-mad with worry, and also with grief over losing his dad. So, it wasn't long before her health began to fail, too, and the boys were terrified that she might die and leave them on their own. Well, Christmas-time came around that year and, of course, there were no gifts. Nobody expected that there would be, and that didn't matter. What mattered was whether or not their mother would pull through, and the fear that someone would find out how desperately poor they were and send them away.

Finally, it was Christmas Eve, and the wind began to howl, a terrible fierce wind that brought in sleet first, and then snow. Jack couldn't sleep for worrying, and sometime after midnight, he left the house where his mother and brother lay sleeping, and fought his way through the wind and snow, down to the shore. He told me that he stood there, tempted to just walk into the waves and give up, that very night. He said that the only thing that stopped him was the thought of his mother and brother on their own, and maybe just his brother left alone if their mother should die, too.

Well, so, there he stood. Alone and completely hopeless. And he began to pray like he'd never prayed before. Tears running down his face and as desperate and lost as anyone could possibly be. He stared out into the pounding waves, though really, he could see nothing except blowing snow. Finally, he wiped his face with his coat sleeve, wet from both his tears and the snow. And, when he looked up again, there was a white stallion, calm as you please, standing just a few feet in front of him and watching him. And, he knew right away that this wasn't one of the wild horses, because this horse's mane and tail lay still, untouched by the merciless winter wind.

He said that he and the horse just stared at each other for what might have been minutes, or even hours, and then the horse just faded away, right before his eyes. Jack said it was odd, but he had felt comforted by the horse, like maybe that stallion had been sent to reassure him that everything would be okay. He didn't understand it, but he suddenly felt a whole lot better, like there was maybe some hope, after all. So, Jack went back to the house, wrapped up in his blankets, and slept like a baby for the rest of the night.

When he awoke the next morning, he wondered if he had just dreamed the whole thing. But then, he heard the rattling of the burners on the cook-stove. He hurried into the next room, and there was his mother, right-as-rain, dressed and getting ready to cook oatmeal. He stood there, saying nothing, with his mouth open. But then, she turned and smiled at him.

"Morning, Jack," was all she said, and then she openly laughed.

He stood looking at her with his mouth still open, but no words would come.

"I know," she finally said. "I can't believe it either, but I woke up this morning feeling fine and plenty-well enough to fix us something to eat." She paused then and turned her face away. "There won't be no special Christmas dinner, though."

Jack crossed the room and threw his arms around her. "It don't matter at all, Momma," he answered. She hugged him back and they both cried. All that day he felt at peace, though he still had no idea about how to make things work so that they could all stay together and in their home.

The blizzard continued the rest of that day and into the next. But, by the following night, all was quiet and calm again. And, by the next morning, the sea was calm too,and Jack and his little brother bundled up and went outside to dig out from the snow as best they could. He told me that the sky was blue and there wasn't a cloud in sight.

The boys worked on and off all that day, and when night settled in again, Jack took another walk down to the shore. He told himself that the horse had appeared to him because his mother was sick, and the fact that she seemed well again was more than he could have hoped for, and that was probably the end of it. He knew that he wasn't likely to ever see that horse again. Still, he wanted to. And, not just because the little family still needed help, but because he'd witnessed a miracle and wanted the reassurance that it had actually

happened; that he had, indeed, seen the Ghost Horse.

Night deepened, and Jack's mother called to him to come back inside. He

answered that he was fine, and that he just wanted to walk by the shore a little

longer before turning in for the night. At this point, he still hadn't told her about

seeing the Ghost Horse. He knew that he would eventually tell her, but for now,

he just couldn't bring himself to say anything for fear that she might expect

more than what might happen.

Eventually, as he walked by the shore and stood for periods of time,

Jack's thoughts went back to trying to figure out what to do. But, like always,

those thoughts flowed in impossible circles without resolution. Finally, in his

weariness, he sat down at the edge of the shore, and not too long after, caught

himself drifting off to sleep. So, he quickly roused himself. He knew very well that

he would freeze to death if he slept outside in the wintry night. He got up,

brushed the snow and sand off his clothes, and rubbed his eyes. But, when he

turned around for one last look at the shore, he stumbled in surprise. Because,

there at the very edge of the shore, stood the Ghost Horse, once again!

Jack said that they looked directly into each other's eyes and then the

horse dropped his graceful head toward the sand, and Jack saw something lying

directly in front of the horse's nose. When he stepped forward to see what it was, the horse disappeared. But, the object did not. He bent to pick it up and saw that it was his dad's old pipe. The one he'd lost a couple of months before he died.

At this point, Jack was no longer sleepy. He raced for the house as fast as his feet would carry him through the slippery, snow-and-ice-packed sand.

"Mother!" he cried. And, she came running, as did Eli. Once they realized that Jack was fine, they sat down close to the stove and listened while he told them everything. About the Ghost Horse, about their mother getting well right after he'd first seen the horse, and about the miraculous reappearance of the lost pipe.

"It's a sign, Jack," his mother declared. She nodded toward the pipe and brought her thin, work-reddened fist down hard, onto the table.

"It's a sign—and he brought something from your dad—so it's a sign from him, too. Maybe he's still able to look out for us, even though he can't be here with us anymore," she said.

Neither of the boys answered; they were both wondering if she might be right, and were almost afraid to hope that she was. It seemed too good to be true. Finally, their mother spoke again. Her voice was firm and they knew that she did not share their doubts.

"We're being looked out for. We just need to wait and the answer will come," she said. *By the time she had pushed herself up and out of her chair, a radiant smile lit her tired face.*

Jack, on the other hand, began to wish that he'd kept quiet, and wondered if he should have told them anything about the horse, at all. What if nothing more happened? What if finding the pipe was just a coincidence and the horse really hadn't "brought" it to him, at all?

Hugh paused from his story-telling and drank the rest of his hot chocolate. He also looked around at his audience. Kate's eager, glowing eyes met his. Zoe stared at her folded hands in her lap, and Sarah's expression was serious. In fact, her pale complexion seemed even more pale than usual. Hugh was reminded that, aside from Sarah, he knew nothing whatever about these people. But, he sat his empty cup down, and continued.

Two weeks later, Jack was still worried and pretty much convinced that nothing further was going to happen. It hurt him to see his mother's watchful, hopeful eyes. He didn't want her, or Eli, for that matter, to be hurt any more than they'd already been. Just when he'd nearly given up hope for the second time, the letter arrived.

In those days, people in Corolla had to pick up their own mail from a post office, and receiving and claiming mail in Corolla during the 1920s could be virtually impossible in bad weather. There were no paved roads then, either.

However, once the snow let up and enough thawing allowed Jack to make the

trip, he walked the necessary miles to the post office and found a letter waiting

there for his mother.

It was postmarked December 8, so had likely been sitting at the post

office a good while before Christmas. Jack could see that the letter was from his

mother's brother, his uncle Jack, for whom he'd been named. Well, he knew that

she would welcome it, and that it might even take her mind off the heavy

business of waiting for the miracle that might or might not manifest. He stuck it

in his pocket, allowed himself the luxury of warming up a little, then began the

long journey back home.

The walk back seemed even longer because the wind had risen and the

sky threatened more snow. Jack was anxious, lest he be caught out and

potentially lost in a blizzard. He walked as fast as he could, and watched the sky

every step of the way. When he was about three-quarters of the way home, the

snow began and he quickened his pace, even more. But, just as the snow fell

faster and thicker, and began to sting his face in earnest, he saw a lamp burning

in the kitchen window of his home and ran the rest of the way. His mother was

anxiously watching for him and opened the door, but before she could say

anything, he handed her the letter and paced around the kitchen until he could breathe normally again. Once she'd helped him take off his wet jacket and boots, and placed them near the stove to dry, she eagerly tore open the damp envelop. A piece of paper fluttered out and fell to the floor.

Jack snatched it up, eagerly looked at it, and cried, "It's a check!" And, sure enough, it was a substantial check; enough to sustain the little family for quite a while, if they were careful.

By this time, Jack's mother's hands were shaking and she found it difficult to unfold the letter that had been wrapped around the check. Meanwhile, Eli was jumping up and down in excitement, and Jack laid a steadying hand on his shoulder as their mother read aloud. The gist of the letter was this:

Uncle Jack had long-since taken over their father's small, one-man, shipping business in Charleston, South Carolina. Over the years, Uncle Jack had built up the business and was doing quite well for himself. In fact, according to the letter, he now owned four boats and had a crew of eight men working for him. And, he was running cargo between South Carolina, North Carolina, and even Virginia.

When Jack's mother finished reading the letter aloud to them, she told them more about their grandfather and how he had only ever had one, small boat that he used to delivered goods to the ports that were located fairly close to home.

The sad news was that she had not seen her own father since she'd married and gone to live in the North Carolina Outer Banks with the boys' father. There had never been enough money to travel home again to visit, and she felt badly about that. She had received word of his death four months earlier, and had told the boys at that time, how much she regretted that they had never had the opportunity to meet their grandfather.

Uncle Jack explained in his letter, that he was sending what he figured their father's estate was worth. He wrote that he was doing well for himself and didn't really need the money, and, he figured that she might need it, badly, with her husband gone. Jack's mother sighed over the letter and told the boys that she believed that her brother had very likely sent them a good bit more money than her father's estate was worth. He had always been a good brother to her, and was known to be a generous man to all who knew him.

But, then they returned to another interesting point in his letter. Uncle Jack said that he had never trusted banks, and he advised his sister to keep her money hidden in her home instead, just as he did. He said that he had purchased a small safe for his home, and recommended that she do the same, or to at least buy a strong, steel box to keep her money in. And, of course, to hide either the *box or the safe, well. As you know, that turned out to be very good advice,*

considering that the banks went under and people lost everything in the Great

Depression that followed. And so, luckily, the little family took Uncle Jack's

advice and were fine when the hard times came.

As to the Ghost Horse, well, Jack saw him just one more time, and that

was the night that the check arrived. Ever since the horse had first appeared,

Jack had kept a steady lookout for him, and was back on the edge of the shore

when, for the last time, the stallion appeared out of the night-mist. The horse

shook his proudly arched neck and, as before, looked directly into Jack's eyes.

Jack said that that night, he spoke to the horse in the mist, hoping, willing, the

stallion to understand how grateful he was—how grateful they all were.

"Thank you." He bowed, and his voice trembled. Then, just as suddenly

as the horse had appeared, he faded away and was not seen again by either

Jack or his family, though, of course, they all kept watch for a very long time and

always hoped to see him. And, that's the happy ending.

Kate sighed, and Zoe's rocking chair creaked as she sat up straight.

Sarah had fallen asleep, and Woolf, sitting close to Zoe's chair, raised his head

and growled down deep in his throat.

"What is it?" Kate asked, jumping up abruptly.

"I don't know, Honey," her mother answered, and motioned at her to be quiet. A loud, scratching sound was coming from the vicinity of their front porch. Hugh motioned them both to be quiet, and carefully listened. Finally, he whispered, "Zoe, go switch off the light. But first, you girls..." he motioned at Kate who was gently shaking Sarah awake, "you go upstairs first, then Zoe, turn off the lamp and follow them."

They obeyed his instructions, though the girls opted to sit in the dark on the top step, out of sight, just in case anything exciting might happen. Zoe stood still, on the step just below them. Hugh stood quietly beside the door, listening, with Woolf, still growling, close beside him.

The sound grew louder, and to all of them, it was the impossible sound of branches scratching the front windows, though there were no branches, no trees or bushes that reached as high as the windows in the front. Hugh tiptoed to the foot of the steps, and whispered.

"Zoe, I'm going out through the back door, but first I need to know if it creaks when you open it."

She paused and whispered, "I don't think so."

"Well then, let's hope not," he replied. But, whatever happens, do *not* let Woolf out and above all, do *not* follow me. If I need back-up, I'll call for it. Just stay where you are and I'll be back as soon as I can."

With that, Hugh drew his gun from its holster and quietly moved through the kitchen. He soundlessly opened the back door, slid through, and closed it again. The waxing moon was higher in the sky now, but was still partially masked by swift-moving clouds. There was very little light, so he easily stayed in the shadows, close against the side of the house. Before he had made much progress though, Woolf's vicious bark exploded the otherwise silent night.

For a split second, his heart felt as though it might pound through his chest, but he quickly recovered and broke into a run. By the time he reached the front of the house, no one was there, and neither was the branch or whatever had been used to create the scratching sounds.

Hugh could vaguely see footprints, but whoever had been there had very likely and deliberately dragged their feet through the sand so that the prints were worthless. And, even in their hurry to leave, they had done the same. Whoever was behind this, Hugh decided, had planned it well.

He walked around the house several times, with his gun still drawn, just in case. But, no one was there, and Woolf had long-since stopped barking. Hugh stood quietly beside the back door, listened for a few minutes longer, and then went back inside and dead-bolted the door behind him. Zoe stood beside the front door, in the dark, with Woolf close beside her. Kate had also cautiously crept back down and was standing at the foot of the steps, gripping the newel post, while Sarah remained seated on the top step.

"Whoever was here is gone; Woolf must have scared them away." He pushed his revolver back into its holster and glanced at Kate, whose eyes registered a combination of fear and defiance. He half-smiled at her, realizing that she had crept downstairs because she didn't want to leave her mother alone.

His voice was gruff, but they knew that he was speaking from his own sense of relief and concern. Then, he chuckled and pointed at the stairs. "Did I tell you girls to stay upstairs? What if somebody had been out there with a gun, waiting for you to come close to the windows or even open the door?" He shook his head.

"Well, they didn't," Zoe answered. "I didn't like to think of you out there all alone, in case something did happen."

"On the other hand," he looked directly into her eyes and spoke slowly, for emphasis. "I do this for a living, and I'm not exactly an idiot. Believe me, I can take care of myself."

Zoe shook her head and swallowed her retort. After all, the man was trying to protect them, which she appreciated, especially now that they were completely on their own. Unexpected tears rose in her eyes, and she quickly blinked them back. Thankfully, Hugh appeared not to notice, and pursued his train of thought.

"I don't like this, Zoe, but there's nothing more I can do right now. Just keep everything locked up and pay close attention to Woolf." He bent and caressed the dog's head. "He'll definitely let you know if anyone is out there."

Zoe, who had by this time, resumed her seat in the rocking chair, got up and followed him to the door. There was no fear in her voice when she spoke. "You know, it was probably nothing more serious than just some kids playing a prank on the out-of-towners. I'm sure that everything is fine, and that we'll be okay. And, we will keep everything secured, even on the second floor, for tonight."

Hugh rubbed a hand across his eyes and asked, "Do you own a gun? And if so, did you bring it with you?"

"No, and no, again," She replied with raised eyebrows. "I guess we've relied on Woolf to protect us, and we plan to just keep doing that."

"Okay, well," he gestured, "again, I'm only a couple of houses away. If anything else happens, call me. It doesn't matter what time it is, just call." He wondered though if she really would, and added, "I mean it. I'm not leaving here until you promise."

Zoe smiled at his earnestness. "Yes—I promise. Now go home and sleep; I'm sure everything is fine. I still think it was just some local kids playing a prank. Maybe your ghost story just had us all in the right mood to believe it was something more."

Hugh shook his head. "Maybe so, and maybe I'm over-reacting, except that, as I've told you, some funny stuff has already been going on at this house. And, I think it's better to over-cautious."

Chapter Ten

Later in the night, after everyone had gone to sleep, Kate was woken by what sounded like something sharply hitting the side of the house. At first she thought that, perhaps, she had dreamed the sound, but then she heard it again. Woolf, asleep in his customary place beside her bed, sat up and growled.

She lay quietly, wondering if she should wake her mother. But time passed and soon the only sound she heard was that of the rhythmic surf outside. Eventually, Kate threw back her bed covers and, as quietly as possible, got up to look out of the window. She glanced back at Sarah, who seemed to be deeply asleep, and cautiously unlocked and raised it, in spite of her mother's instructions to leave all the windows locked.

At first, she stood deeply breathing in the chilly, night air and looking up at the starry sky. But then, she noticed something shadowy that moved slowly along the shore. After a few moments, it disappeared and Kate turned back to her bed before remembering that she needed to close and lock the window again. As she came back to do so, she noticed something else. It was a dim, whitish-glow just at the edge of the shore.

Though she stood as close to the window as possible, she couldn't quite make out what it was at first. She also wondered if, from where she stood, she might be seen by someone looking toward the house. However, she realized that her window was now in shadow, and besides, the moon's frail light would hardly be a threat. Still, she glanced down, thankful for her dark-colored pajamas and confident that she was invisible to anyone outside.

Having resolved that issue to her satisfaction, she looked back toward the shore, and as her eyes re-adjusted to the darkness before her, the dim glow that she'd seen earlier began to take form. She gasped, afraid to breathe. Surely, it was a white horse that she saw! It must be—it had to be—the very same Ghost Horse that Hugh had just told them about. After all, he had also said that there were no white horses living on Corolla anymore, so what else could it be? The horse, or whatever it was, appeared to turn and face her house, and she had the uncanny feeling that he could see her there, looking out of her window, in spite of the shadows and the darkness, and her pajamas.

Only moments later, the horse faded, or at least, Kate was pretty sure that it had faded. By this time, she was also fairly confident that what she had seen was the Ghost Horse, but there was, of course, there was always the possibility that whatever it was had simply walked away into the vast darkness. A tiny doubt remained in her mind. She had never thought much about ghosts one way or the other, and this seemed like a huge coincidence, considering she had just learned about this particular horse a couple of hours earlier. And, if it was the Ghost Horse, did she and her mother actually need help of some kind?

As far as Kate knew, Zoe discussed most things with her, but she supposed there was always a possibility that she was not aware of everything that went on in their lives. She was disconcerted by that thought, but eventually, her sleepiness won out and she snuggled under the covers. Sometime in the night, she dreamed that many horses were surrounding her house in order to guard something. In the dream though, she couldn't see what it was that they were guarding, and didn't know why they were there. By morning, she shrugged the dream off, and blamed her obsession with the Ghost Horse for it.

Chapter Eleven

Morning brought dark-clouded skies and mist. No one mentioned the previous night's events and, in fact, they were all quieter than usual, but perhaps that was due to the darkened, morning skies. After breakfast, Zoe gathered up the dirty dishes and announced that they would be making another trip back to Corolla. She had decided to buy a few things from the *Corolla Wild Horse Fund* shop and maybe visit the village store again, as well.

Kate asked for another glass of orange juice and lingered in the kitchen after Sarah went upstairs to get dressed. But really, she just wanted to talk privately with her mother.

"Mom," she hesitated, and tugged at her hair as she typically did when she was feeling anxious, "is everything okay?" she scanned her mother's surprised face. Zoe's eyebrows lifted, but before she could ask what was behind that question, Kate breathlessly confessed, "I saw the Ghost Horse standing on the edge of the shore last night."

Immediate disbelief, and then quick anger, crossed Zoe's face. She rested one hand on her hip and gripped the dishtowel tightly in the other, as she attempted to calm herself. But, her attempt was less than successful.

"Oh, for heaven's sake, Kate! She exploded. Then, in a quieter voice, she muttered, "I should never have allowed him to tell you that stupid story. I was afraid of something like this." She angrily tossed the dishtowel onto the table. "I'll have a talk with him today."

"No—please, Mom," Kate begged. "It's not his fault and if something really is wrong, we might need him. Besides, I'm telling you the truth. I got up in the night and saw what I'm pretty sure was the Ghost Horse standing at the edge of the water. "

Zoe snatched up the dish towel again and tightened her lips into a thin line.

"I mean it, Mom," Kate's voice rose in desperation. "I wouldn't lie to you. I saw him!"

"That's enough, Kate!" she shouted, and turned back to the sink. "I don't want to hear *any* more about it, do you hear me?"

Kate, who was furious and frustrated, stamped her foot. "I don't understand you! Why can't you believe in anything? Dad would have; he'd have believed me. He'd have believed in the Ghost Horse and he would have told you so!" Tears flowed down her reddened cheeks.

Zoe whipped around to face her and abruptly answered, "Well, we'll never know, will we? You have no idea what he would have said or done."

'I know just as well as you do what he would have said or done," Kate fired back. She, too, shouted as she turned and fled from the room. "Sometimes I really hate you, and sometimes I just wish I was dead, too!"

Deeply stung, Zoe watched Kate disappear down the hall. With shaking hands, she poured herself another cup of coffee, sank into the nearest chair and put her head down on her arms. How-on-earth was she supposed to cope with this child on her own? Unreasonable anger rose up in her toward her dead husband, as though he had deliberately left them. But, just as quickly, the anger was replaced by despair. They should never have come to this place. But, she'd already paid to rent the house for two weeks, and so they would stay. And then what? That was the Big Question, she knew.

Sarah was brushing her hair when Kate rushed back into the bedroom they shared and slammed the door. Their eyes met briefly in the large mirror before Sarah carefully looked away, and then Kate realized that Sarah had heard her, and her mother, shouting at one another. Truthfully, Kate acknowledged, there was no way that she couldn't have heard their shouting, and she instantly regretted it. She didn't know what to say or do, so she sat down on the edge of the bed.

Chapter Twelve

Sarah, still brushing her hair, brightly asked, "Hey, how about working on our home-schooling stuff together, Kate? I'm working on an English essay right now and need two more pages. What are you working on?"

As Sarah over-enthusiastically chatted about her essay without waiting for Kate to answer, Kate knew that she was only trying to avoid referencing the unpleasantness that she'd overheard downstairs. Besides which, by this time, Sarah had brushed her hair so much that it was nearly standing on-end from static electricity.

Aside from noticing the strange state of Sarah's hair, Kate was, at that moment, unable to focus. She sat on the bed and absently pulled at a loose piece of thread on the bedspread. Finally, unable to bear Sarah's chatter anymore, she abruptly jumped up and suggested that they take a walk along the shore. Sarah's shoulders slumped in obvious relief as she carefully laid her hairbrush down on the dresser and scooted her feet into her dirty sneakers. The girls were much quieter than usual as they walked down the stairs, each nervously clinging to the railing as though it was a life-support system. Part-way down, they heard Zoe close the office door, and then they scooted around the corner and down the hall into the kitchen as fast as they could hurry.

Perhaps it was stress from the argument, but they both agreed that they were hungry again. Sarah reached for paper towels while Kate put four slices of bread into the toaster. They donned their jackets and hats while they waited and, shortly afterward, they crunched buttery, cinnamon toast and shivered together in the cold, morning wind as they made their way toward the shore.

Kate was anxious to look at the place where she estimated the ghost horse had appeared in the night. As strange as it sounded, even to her, she felt that he had waited for her to come to the window and really had seen her, even in the dark. She also wondered, had he somehow summoned her? For a brief moment, she inwardly snorted at the thought. Her mother would undoubtedly say that she was being silly. But secretly, it felt possible to her, and she couldn't help but wish it was true.

The morning clouds scudded wildly in the wind, and clumps of sea oats bent their faces toward the sandy ground. The beach was deserted. The gray-green waves rolled in heavily before crashing down on the shore. There was no gentle lapping this morning. Once they'd reached the water's edge, Kate carefully looked for signs of the horse's night-time appearance while Sarah innocently chattered about her shell-collection and her desire to show them all to Kate.

"And, I'd love to find a fossilized shark's tooth someday," Sarah continued. "I know people around here who have, but they must be rare because I've been looking for a couple of years and still haven't found one." She abruptly spun around and threw her arms out as though dancing to her own, inward music. At least she didn't seem to be upset about the morning's argument anymore, Kate surmised.

"Do you like fossils?" Sarah shouted over the wind. "Have you ever found any? I have a book about them, but haven't read much of it, yet." She began to hum whatever the tune was, in her head.

Kate didn't answer her right away. She was busy examining the shoreline as they walked, or rather, she walked and Sarah danced. Finally, she had to admit to herself that there was no evidence that a horse had stood by the shore. At the same time, she also knew that the tide would have long-since washed away any prints. But still, if she had seen the Ghost Horse, maybe his prints would have magically remained. After all, she had once seen those clear prints with no explanation.

Oddly enough, for reasons that she could neither explain nor understand, the absence of hoof-prints made Kate even more certain that the horse had been there in the night. And, she had no intention of backing down from that belief, whatever her mother might have to say about it.

After all, she thought, a person has a right to believe what they want to believe, even if it differs from everyone else's beliefs. But then she thought of Hugh and anxiously pulled her jacket more tightly around herself.

"Yes, I have a couple of fossils that my dad gave me," she finally answered Sarah. "One is an Indian arrowhead that my grandpa plowed up on his farm in the Midwest, and the other is a leaf that fossilized in some sort of sandstone. My uncle from Oklahoma gave that one to me."

"Cool!" Sarah replied. "I guess you don't have them with you, do you?" Without pausing for an answer, she twisted a strand of hair around one finger, and continued.

"My dad collects things, too, but no fossils that I know of. Anyway, one day, I found an old coin on the kitchen floor and he told me that it was from his collection." She pulled her blowing scarf over her head and tied it tightly under her chin.

"I asked him if I could see the rest of them, and he said that maybe, someday. But, he never got around to showing any of them to me, so maybe I'll ask him, again." With that, Sarah skipped on down the shore, only pausing here and there to pick up shells that drew her attention.

Kate was fine with that; she was relieved to be able to focus on her own thoughts. She really hoped that Zoe wouldn't argue with Hugh for telling them about the Ghost Horse, in the first place. She actually liked him and wanted him to come back to the house, and that thought surprised her, as well.

In a flash, it came to her that last night was the first time since her father's death that they had had any visitors, or that she had seen her mother really laugh. She wanted to feel safe and to be comfortable, again. And, she wanted to feel like they were a family once again, too. Then, another wave of uneasiness swept over her. What if Hugh blamed her for Zoe's anger? Frustration gripped her, and she gritted her teeth at the wind and impatiently kicked at the sand, then deliberately took a deep breath to quiet herself. That was usually a good idea, except that it didn't work this time.

The only sounds that the girls could hear were those of the wind, the rustling sea oats, the occasional cries of sea-birds, and the unending sweep of the tide, which was growing more agitated as it pounded the shore. The scudding clouds were becoming darker, as were the rising waves. Kate cupped her hands and called to Sarah that they should go in. But, at that very moment, they heard Zoe shouting over the wind. They soon found themselves just opposite the house, but were still too far away to understand what Zoe was saying. Both turned to wave at her and began moving away from the shore. However, as they drew closer to the house, they simultaneously stopped and bumped into each other, and then gasped in unison as they could see past Zoe and at the siding on the front porch, behind her.

Zoe was smiling at them, so they knew that she hadn't seen it, yet. Their anxious eyes met, and then Kate took off running as fast as she could against the heavy resistance of the sand, with Sarah pelting close behind her. When Kate judged that they were near enough to be heard, she pushed back her blowing hair and shouted, "Mom!" and pointed at the house. Zoe turned to look at what they were pointing at, and then she sagged against the porch railing as though all of her strength had suddenly abandoned her. There, on the porch wall, were bright-red, spray-painted words that said, *"Leave now or die."*

Both girls reached the porch at the same time and pounded up the steps, breathing hard. Kate's thoughts were only for her mother, and she threw her arms around Zoe, who was, quite literally, speechless. In fact, for a few moments, she could only lean against the railing and stare at the message on the ruined wall. She was barely aware of the frightened girls who huddled close against her, waiting for her to speak, to act, to somehow reassure them that everything was all right.

Finally, out of the wind-blown silence, Sarah began to cry and the sound brought Zoe back to the present moment. She stood up straight and looked down at the girls as though surprised to see them there, with her. First, she gave Kate a quick, reassuring hug, and then gathered Sarah into her arms.

"Hush, Sarah; there's nothing to be afraid of. This is probably just somebody's bad idea of a joke!" She gently rocked Sarah back and forth in her arms. "Come on; there is nothing to worry about. I promise. Woolf would never let anything happen to us." She looked up at Kate.

"Honey, will you get Sarah some tissues, and grab my cell phone on your way back out here?"

"Sure, Mom," said Kate, who was relieved to have something to do. She raced into the house and returned laden with a box of tissues and Zoe's phone, into which Hugh had insisted on programming his cell number the night before.

He answered on the second ring and said that he would come right away. Meanwhile, neither Zoe nor the girls wanted to go back inside, so they settled down together on the top step, and waited. None of them spoke because there didn't seem to be anything to say. About 20-minutes later, a Currituck County police-cruiser pulled up and Hugh climbed out from the passenger side. His easy-going smile was missing as he hurried over to where they waited. Zoe sat between Kate and Sarah, who were huddled against either side of her. Hugh's eyes met hers, and she gestured at the wall behind them.

"We were surprised, to say the least," she said. Then she added, "I suppose this is the work of whoever was out here last night?"

"I would assume so," he answered. "But, it would be hard to be absolutely certain about that."

Zoe put her hand up to her throat. "You know, at the time, I thought that you were just over-reacting to those scratching sounds we heard, but I don't think that anymore. I mean, this looks," she waved her hand at the painted words behind her, "pretty serious to me."

She slowly rose to her feet and reached for the railing. "Honestly, I'd really looked forward to spending some time here. But, under the circumstances, now, I think we'd better just leave." She abruptly let go of the railing again and folded her arms. Hugh waited for her to say more, but she didn't. She turned away from him and faced the sea with a thoughtful look in her eyes.

Hugh squared his shoulders and stepped in front of her, forcing her to look at him. His voice was that of a law-enforcement professional's when he spoke. "I completely understand, but I'd like you to stay at least another day or two. Right now, we're going to look around for clues and take a couple of photos. And, I promise you that I *will* get to the bottom of this, no matter what." His eyes were angry.

Zoe looked up at him and nodded. "Well, you can probably do that with us out of the way." She continued, "We can't tell you much because we didn't see it until right before I called you. But ask us anything that you want and we'll cooperate. Tell me though, we are free to leave when we want to, aren't we?"

Hugh nodded and gritted his teeth impatiently. "Yes. I can't make you stay, but I wish you would at least give me a day or two because if you stay, we may be able to sort this out more quickly." She shrugged her shoulders in a non-committal way and buttoned her sweater against the wind.

He watched her a moment, then added, "And, we'll certainly do everything we can to protect you while you're here." He started to say something else, then glanced down at the girls and stopped. Instead, he turned and introduced his partner, who waited quietly at the foot of the front steps.

"This is Jake Starling," he said. Jake nodded briefly at Zoe and the girls, then pulled out papers from a zippered-case that he carried, and began to ask questions. Hugh stepped aside, and waited.

But, as Zoe had already said, none of them could offer much information. Not long after, Zoe sent the girls inside while Jake first examined the ground around the front of the house, and then went around to the left side. Zoe reached for the door, but Hugh touched her shoulder and asked,

"Come over here with me, will you?" He gestured in the direction of the car, and she nodded in reply. They walked a short distance away from the house, and for a few moments, both watched Jake where he knelt in the sand.

"Look," he uneasily began. He could feel himself blushing. "I didn't want to say this in front of the girls and it's awkward for me to ask, but I have to. Do you understand?"

Zoe nodded and he continued. "I just want to make sure that what happened here is nothing personal. Because, if you leave here and someone is out to get *you*, *personally*, then you'll be on your own. But, if this happened just because you're staying here, in this house, that's an entirely different matter. I just want to know that it's safe for you to leave before you actually go."

Shock registered on Zoe's face, and her eyebrows shot up. Hugh watched her closely, wanting to believe that whatever she had to say would be the truth. "No one is out to get me," she emphatically stated, "if that's what you mean. Why-on-earth would they be?"

"Okay," he acquiesced, and defensively held up his hands. "I just had to ask."

She expected him to say more, but he abruptly dropped the subject and strode away, intending to take a look at the other side of the house. Zoe considered following him, but then decided that she had had enough and headed for the front door, instead. But she turned around again when she heard Jake shout, "Looks like a ladder might have been here at one point!"

Hugh and Zoe reached the place where Jake knelt in the sand, at the same time. He pointed at what might have been prints made from the base of a ladder, and then all three of them looked up at the house.

"What room is directly up there from this point?" Jake asked.

"I believe I know," Hugh answered. "There's a locked room in the house, and that's the one, right above here."

Jake looked surprised. "You've been in this house?" he asked.

While Hugh hesitated, Zoe cleared her throat. Her voice sounded huskier than usual. "There's one room in the house that is locked. We were told that the owner keeps his own things in there and that's really all we know. We didn't think much about it one way or the other. There's a combination lock on that door," she added.

Jake was thoughtful for a moment, then looked at Hugh. "Do you think we could get a search-warrant?"

Hugh rubbed his chin. "Now that a threat has been issued, I think we may be able to do that, although no one has suffered actual, physical harm. But, the problem is that meanwhile, if the owner is up to something, he might be desperate to move whatever is in there, and I don't want these folks to be in any more danger. We're going to need to be really careful about how we handle this."

Jake nodded thoughtfully, and Hugh asked Zoe about her plans for the day. She explained that their intention had been to make the trip back to Corolla. He nodded, his eyes on the ground, and said, "Go on ahead."

"There's no point in your sitting around here. We'll stay a little while longer, but you go on. There's nothing you can do here, anyway." He looked up at the lead-gray sky. "Looks like a storm could eventually blow in," he added. "Be careful; you don't want to get caught out in it, if you can help it. Driving on this beach without a road can be more than tough, depending on the weather."

Suddenly, he frowned and met her eyes. "Are you going to take Woolf with you?"

"No," she answered. "I was going to leave him here unless you think I should bring him along for some reason."

"No," Hugh spoke emphatically. "Definitely leave him at home because I'd feel a whole lot better if he was here in the house to keep an eye on things. By the way, how long do you think you'll be gone?"

"I don't know," Zoe shrugged. "Maybe an hour and a half, maybe not even that. She crossed her arms and sighed. "Are you sure it's okay to leave?"

"Yes. Look, you're not a prisoner here, and you can't just sit in the house and wait for something to happen. I'll talk to you again later this afternoon." His voice was still professional and reassuring, but his blue eyes mirrored his personal concern.

Not long after, he watched them climb into the Jeep and as they drove away, he waved at the girls, who anxiously waved back. Then, he walked over to his partner.

"Well, Jake, what do *you* think?"

Jake, who had continued to examine the ground, suddenly stood up with an amused look on his face. "So, this is your new neighbor, Hugh? You seem to be pretty well acquainted with her already," he teased.

Hugh glared, and Jake abruptly changed his tone. "All kidding aside, Hugh, what do you know about these people? Is there any chance that this woman *might* be in on whatever is going on?"

Hugh shoved his hands in his pockets and looked away without answering. Jake watched him closely, then shrugged and added, "Okay, maybe not. You've been saying for a while that something is wrong here. But, either this woman is in on whatever is going on, or she's very likely in for more trouble."

When Hugh didn't answer, he added, "But, you already know that, don't you?"

"Hard to say which," Hugh tersely admitted.

Chapter Thirteen

A few horses stood quietly up on a ridge of dunes as Zoe drove toward Corolla, but none were close by, or at the water's edge. The girls were unusually quiet and observed them without comment. Zoe, who had been lost in her own thoughts, mentally shook herself. She had finally registered the girls' lack of conversation, and made a hearty attempt to restore some feeling of normalcy to the day.

"Hey, girls," her voice was too loud. Too enthusiastic. "Should we stop at *Aunt Susie's* again and pick up something different for lunch?"

Sarah murmured, "I don't care."

Kate's voice was toneless. "Me, either. I don't really care, Mom."

"Okay." Zoe decided to not push for a decision at that moment. "Well, while we're thinking about that, let's visit the *Corolla Wild Horse Fund Museum Store* again before we do anything else. I want to pick up a couple of things there."

Neither girl replied. Shortly afterward, Zoe pulled into an empty parking space in front of the building, and they went inside. Another young woman was behind the counter this time, and she smiled as they walked in. She introduced herself as Stella, and easily chatted with the girls, whom, Zoe noted, seemed to cheer up quickly. In fact, not many minutes later, Zoe marveled as she heard them giggling together. "I guess kids really are resilient," she observed to herself, and then proceeded to take her time looking around the Shop.

In the end, she selected a hoodie for each of the girls, and an elegant shawl for herself. Then, she picked up a book with a beautiful cover that told the history of the wild horses.

They were all feeling much better by the time Zoe deposited her purchases on the counter to pay for them. The girls were pleased with their new hoodies, and Kate pounced on the book.

"Oh, Mom! Is this for me?" she asked. Her eyes, so recently troubled, were glowing.

Zoe looked at her daughter's anxious face and didn't have the heart to say that she had intended to buy the book for herself. "I'll tell you what, Kate," she smiled. "I'll buy a copy of this book for each of us, including you and Sarah. It'll be a nice reminder of our time together, here at Corolla."

Kate replied by grinning at her mother, but Sarah's smile wobbled a little. "I'd never forget you, even without the book and the hoodie."

"Oh, dear," thought Zoe. She was already more than a little worried about leaving Sarah behind, and she also knew that they would need to leave her, maybe very soon. But, for the moment, she pushed those concerns to the back of her mind and quickly hugged Sarah, then released her and pulled a credit card from her wallet.

"Oh," Stella said, as she rang up the books, "I *guarantee* that you'll love this book, and that you'll never think of the horses quite the same way again, either. They are *so, so* special, and not just because I work here," she added.

Chapter Fourteen

A strong scent of coffee greeted them as the screen door that opened into Old Village Store slammed shut behind them. Just as before, Rose Hoskins was there, with a smile on her face. But, this time, she was already standing behind the counter. She shut the cash register drawer with a bang, and deftly handed change to an elderly customer.

"Hi, Ladies!" she called to them. "What can I help you with, today?" Rose was a friendly, outgoing woman and they couldn't help but grin back at her. But, just as Zoe opened her mouth to answer, a small, claw-like hand reached from behind and clutched her elbow. "Hello, again, dear!" said the eager voice.

Startled, Zoe swung around and looked down at the small, older woman whose gleaming, dark eyes looked eagerly up into her own. For a split second, she acquiesced to the woman's surprisingly strong grip, but then, in a not-so-gentle manner, tugged her own arm away.

"I met you on the beach yesterday morning, dear," the little woman persisted, as she vainly attempted to grab hold of Zoe's arm, again.

"By the way, I'm Susan Hall, and I'm really glad to have bumped into you again." The woman's smile was friendly, but Zoe didn't answer. She was too busy trying to form a quick escape plan that wouldn't look too obviously rude.

"Don't you remember?" the older woman persisted, as she abandoned her attempt to grab Zoe's arm, and reached for her shoulder, instead. She slightly shook Zoe, as though attempting to jog her memory. "I'm the one who told you that I'd seen the Ghost Horse!"

"Yes," Zoe muttered. Susan turned to Rose with excitement and conviction in her voice. "Did I tell you that I'd seen him, Rosie? He's back, and I just wonder what's going to happen next. Isn't it exciting?"

Susan Hall positioned herself so that she directly faced Zoe. "He was opposite your house, dear, so maybe he's come to see you." She nodded her encouragement, though Zoe's eyes only expressed shock and outrage.

"Are you, by chance, in any trouble?" Susan cheerfully persisted.

"Not at all," was Zoe's cutting reply. She deliberately turned away to examine the small stacks of chewing gum and candy on the counter, and Susan Hall relinquished the struggle, having apparently accepted defeat. She chatted with Rose for a few minutes more about the Ghost Horse, then cheerfully called "Good-bye" to all of them, and waved as she headed out the door.

Rose observed Zoe's disgruntled expression and chuckled. "You musn't mind her; she means well. She's lived here most of her life, just like me. In fact, we were in school together, and she's always been what you might call a little unusual." Zoe looked unconvinced.

"But she means well," Rose persisted, and Zoe's frown deepened.

Rose tried once more. "Susan believes that she can see some things that other people can't. Then again, maybe she can; who's to say?" Rose's voice grew thoughtful. "But, as far as the Ghost Horse is concerned, I do believe that he is real. People have seen him over the years, and not just Susan," she mused. "So maybe something *is* about to happen," she shrugged. "Not that it's going to happen to you," she quickly added. "That may not be the case at all, so try not to worry about it."

Kate held her breath as she waited for her mother's response. But, Zoe just quietly gathered up the groceries she wanted from the shelves, while Rose tactfully changed the subject to the weather and the overall rising costs of her merchandise. Zoe eventually forced herself to respond to Rose's small-talk, but she only half-listened to what was said, and mechanically answered "yes" or "no" at what she hoped were the appropriate moments.

By the time they left the store, Zoe really was feeling calmer, and she and the girls agreed that they would order additional chicken barbeque to take home with them, after all. And so, once again, they had the opportunity to admire the well-developed ambience and social skills of the resident hens, Lucy and Ethel, which made them all laugh in spite of their worries.

During the time they had been shopping, the dark sky had grown even darker, and a few drops of rain fell by the time Zoe turned away from the paved road and onto the sand. Driving fast on the beach is not a legal option, and right before they reached the house, the wind dramatically rose and gathered loose sand up into the air, held it for a moment, and then slammed it back to the ground.

Hard, slate-gray rain immediately followed. It plummeted from the sky just as they pulled into the driveway and reached the shelter underneath the house, where the rain sharply pounded the metal roof. The girls dashed up the steep steps to the front porch with Zoe at their heels. And, a moment later, they all pushed their way into the front hall. Zoe slammed and locked the door behind them and everyone quickly kicked off their wet shoes and removed their jackets. The girls headed for the stairs, but Zoe stopped them.

"I don't know about you, but I need something hot to drink with our lunch. What about it?"

"Yes, please!" they both agreed, and shivered as they followed her to the kitchen. Zoe grabbed a tin of cocoa and a bag of sugar from the cupboard nearest the stove, retrieved the milk from the refrigerator, and poured the mixture into a pan on the stove. Then, she turned to look at them. "Go get your wet jackets and put them in the dryer while we're eating."

Once that was done and the hot chocolate and barbeque was equally distributed, everyone settled down at the table. But, Kate couldn't sit still. She jumped right back up and went to look out the kitchen window. "You can't see anything, Mom, not even the houses nearby," she exclaimed.

"Are we still going to bake cookies again," Sarah anxiously asked. "I guess I'd better go home when it clears up, unless we're going to bake cookies, that is."

"Yes," Zoe chuckled. "You can go home afterwards if you want to. But Sarah," she paused, "if your dad is still not at home, you can come back here, you know. Have dinner and spend the night with us again."

Sarah looked relieved and grinned back at her. "I'll do that. And, maybe if he's there, I'll come back anyway."

Chapter Fifteen

Hugh McKenzie's thoughts were troubled by the twin possibilities that whatever was happening at the Owens house was even more sinister than he had initially supposed, and also that Zoe might actually have some knowledge of it that she was hiding. He wondered if the spray-painted threat was a ruse to gain his sympathy and allow her time to get out and away. If she was involved, or at least had knowledge of it...he could hardly allow himself to finish that thought. He also knew that he might well have been a fool to confess any of his own suspicions and observations to her.

On the other hand, he reasoned, he had taken a chance because he needed to start somewhere with this investigation. But, he hadn't told her everything he knew, either. Such as, his suspicion that Sarah's step-father might be involved, and that the locked room housed either smuggled goods or perhaps even people, at times.

Hugh pursed his lips and unconsciously shook his head. Privately, he hoped she was innocent. He acknowledged that he was attracted to Zoe, but also coolly acknowledged that fact as a weakness to be constantly mindful of, because he needed to remain as emotionally detached as possible.

"Damn," he audibly snorted, and brought his hand down hard on the steering wheel in front of him. Aside from his personal feelings, his gut-feelings still told him that she knew nothing about any of this. Or, he asked himself, do I just feel that way because I want that to be the truth?

He wondered if she would try to leave and, somehow, he needed to stop her from doing that without telling her why. The day was still young and he already felt exhausted. But, he stubbornly set his jaw without realizing that he'd done so. He knew his duty, and he would do it, no matter what.

Once back at the station, Hugh asked Jake to run a background check on Zoe while he began working to track-down Graham Owens in Washington D.C. It took a little while to do so, and Hugh noted that the day seemed to be passing much more slowly than usual. In the end though, he found what he needed, and Graham, who was not at work, but was attending a conference in Canada instead, answered his cell phone on the first ring.

An hour later, Hugh went to get a cup of coffee and to find Jake. "Have you got anything yet?" he asked.

Jake stood up from his desk and stretched. "Not yet—you know as well as I do that a thorough check can take a little while. Why? What's going on?"

"Well, have a seat," Hugh's eyebrows rose. "You won't want to miss any of this."

Jake sank back into his chair with a sigh, as Hugh pulled up another chair and placed it directly opposite his. He leaned across the desk. "Owens claims that he didn't even know his house was being rented out. It seems that his

museum colleague and friend, Robert Caldwell, has a key to the place and

Owens has told him that he can use the house whenever he wants to. And that's

not all," Hugh paused and sipped his coffee.

"He also says that he, himself, hasn't been out here for nearly a year,

but is planning to come down for Christmas with his family."

Jake's eyes widened. "So, good-old-Robert has rented Owens's house

and is collecting the rent to keep for himself. Sounds to me like he's one heck of

a good friend, don't you think? Remind me never to give the keys to my house

to a "friend," will you?" he snorted.

"Yeah, no kidding. But wait, because there's more," Hugh continued.

"Owens claims to know absolutely nothing about a locked room. He says that he

doesn't keep anything of value in his Corolla house, and so has no need to lock

up any of the rooms."

"Great," Jake groaned. "So, what do we do now?"

"Well, to begin with, Owens isn't in Washington right now. He's a

conference in Vancouver, but he said that he could leave right away and be

down here by tomorrow night."

Jake started to speak, but Hugh held up his hand and continued. "Wait a

minute; let me tell you the rest of it first. I told him not to come. Frankly, we don't need any more innocent people in the middle of this, if at all possible. So, I told him to just stay where he is and I'll keep him up-to-date on everything. He knows that we're watching the house. And now, he also knows that we've *been* watching it for a while."

Hugh shoved his empty coffee cup aside and rested both elbows on Jake's desk.

"By the way, we do have his full permission to search the premises, but, I don't think we should do anything until we have a full report on Zoe. And, either way, we need to somehow keep her from packing up and leaving."

"Why?" Jake leaned back in his chair. "If she's guilty, you know where to find her. And, if she's innocent, you can't use her as bait to help bring in the bad boys, Hugh."

Chapter Sixteen

Later that afternoon, and with more cookies baked, the rain finally slowed to a gentle shower and the doorbell rang. Woolf barked sharply, just once, and Zoe called out, "Who is it?"

"Me," Hugh answered. "Just me."

She opened the door. "Well, your timing is perfect, because we've just finished making another batch of cookies."

Hugh grinned in spite of himself, and followed her to the kitchen where he sat down in a chair next to Kate. Zoe handed him a cup of coffee and he reached for several warm cookies. He asked about their day and admired their purchases, which the girls had immediately gathered up to show to him.

Hugh commented on the rain and talked for a while about the special events and ways that holidays were observed on the Outer Banks. He carefully avoided that which concerned them all, and Zoe did not push him. She knew he would eventually discuss whatever was important with her, but probably not in front of the girls.

The girls seemed reluctant to leave the table though, and finally, Zoe decided to initiate the opportunity for them to talk privately. She was about to suggest that the girls might want to watch a movie, when Kate spoke up.

"Hey, Mom, I'd like to walk Sarah home." Before her mother could respond, Kate continued. "And, I'll be careful and I won't be gone long. Okay?"

"Okay," Zoe nodded. "But, be back here in an hour. I don't want you wandering on your own, just now. In fact, why don't you take Woolf with you?"

Kate made a face because she was feeling brave at that moment, but decided not to push the point with her mother. So, she turned to Sarah, instead. "Hey, do you care if I bring Woolf along?" she asked. "If your dad is there, we won't come inside."

"Okay," Sarah agreed, and Zoe quietly exhaled her relief. The two girls hurriedly rose and went to bundle themselves into their dry jackets and then retrieved their still-damp shoes, while Zoe clipped Woolf's leash firmly onto his collar.

"Be back here in an hour, either way," she ordered.

"Yep," Kate agreed and waved her hand without looking back. But Sarah turned to smile and wave at them both. She was pleased that Kate was walking her home.

The minute the door closed behind them, Zoe resumed her seat at the kitchen table, leaned back, and crossed one blue-jean-clad leg over the other. "Now what?" she questioned Hugh. "And, what did you find out?"

Hugh, who had been quietly observing and admiring her, hesitated. How much could he safely say? In the end, he chose to be cautious and to closely watch her reactions. He looked directly into her eyes. And, Zoe recognized, by the expression in his own eyes, that he was very much a lawman at that moment.

"Do you personally know Graham Owens?" Hugh began.

"No." She shook her head and absently pushed her hair behind one ear. "I've seen him, of course, because I am a museum curator in Virginia and, within the state, including Washington D.C., everyone pretty much knows who everyone else is."

She added, "He's with the National Portrait Gallery, isn't he?"

Instead of answering her question, Hugh proceeded to ask his own. "How did you come to rent this house, then? Was it through Robert Caldwell?"

Zoe patiently confirmed that Robert, being a close friend of Graham's, had asked if she might rent the house for two weeks in order to finish a collections book for the museum. At the same time, being on the Outer Banks would also provide her with a much-needed break from the routines of work and home.

Hugh decided not to tell her that Owens knew nothing about her being there, and continued to ask his questions. "How well do you know Robert Caldwell? Would you say that he a person that you feel you can trust?"

A look of genuine surprise crossed Zoe's face. She sat up straight and and carefully considered her next words. "I work for him. He has a good reputation in the field, and I've come to know him pretty well. So yes, I suppose that I can trust him, at least according to what I know of him. Why?" she added.

Hugh visibly winced as he asked the next uncomfortable question. "Have you ever had reason to suspect him of any illegal activities of any kind?"

Zoe's eyebrows shot up. "Good heavens, no!"

"Okay, so he seems to be pretty above-board. Do you know anything about his friends or his interests?" he persisted.

"Not much," she admitted. "I know that he's a collector of ancient antiquities and has an impressive, personal collection. It's okay though," she quickly added, "because ancient antiquities are not the focus of the museum where we both work, so it doesn't present any professional conflict-of-interest."

A distant alarm-bell sounded in Hugh's mind. He could see a logical connection, but a lot would depend on what she said next. He drew a deep breath and asked, "How ancient? And how does he buy these things for his collection?"

"I'm honestly not sure where they come from," she admitted. "I mean, obviously, they would have to come from somewhere like the Middle East, or Greece, or Rome, originally. But, since that's neither my field of interest nor the focus of my work, I really don't know much about any of it. He has some things in his office..." Zoe left her sentence unfinished. She paused thoughtfully and referred back to his first question.

"You understand that I really don't know much of anything about his private collections?" Her expression was serious and somewhat defiant. But, maybe defensive is a better word, Hugh thought to himself.

Hugh nodded as though he understood. He really didn't want to put her on her guard; he needed her to just tell him whatever she knew. He said, "Just tell me what you do know, or have heard about his private collections."

"Well," she thought for a moment, "he has coins. A lot of different kinds of coins. I know some of them are Roman, some Egyptian, and some are Syrian, because he told me that, once. He also has a few small statues, possibly Roman from the look of them," she shrugged. "They could also be Greek or even Etruscan, for all I know. Honestly, I never paid much attention to them, so I'm really not sure."

She absentmindedly rubbed her cheek. "Oh, and one time he did show me something that he thought might have been an example of early Christian iconography. Was it a horse? I'll have to think about it and try to remember," she sighed.

But, a split-second later, she gasped and sat upright in her chair. Her green eyes blazed and she shook her head. "No—you don't mean…" she began, horrified.

Hugh, unable to hide his mounting excitement any longer, nodded. "If this is what I think it is, I've got him. I've got him and, hopefully, all of his friends, too. Because, there is no way that he could begin to pull this off, on his own."

"But," Zoe stammered, "how-on-earth could he begin to pull off something like this at all? I mean, it would have to include a *lot* of other people. Wouldn't it?" she added.

"Not necessarily," Hugh explained. "He would only need one dealer in the Middle East who might also arrange for a carrier, and then one or two other people on this end. That might be all that the smugglers require, depending on the merchandise that they're moving."

They were both quiet for a few minutes before Hugh continued. "Think about it, Zoe. Everything that you've said he collects, is small and easily hidden. Pretty easily transported, too. We're not talking about anything large at all, are we? Just coins, and pocket-sized statues, and things like that. Right?"

"That's all that I know of," she admitted. "There may be other, larger things. Still," she shook her head, "I can't quite believe that he would do this. I've known him for several years, and I'm having trouble grasping the idea that he might be a smuggler." She frowned. "That would mean that the man I work for is, in fact, a thief. A criminal."

Hugh consciously felt his muscles clench. He knew that it was time to ask her yet another relevant question. He felt his face redden, and forced himself to meet her eyes, though his inclination was to examine the table-top, instead.

"Zoe," he began, "I hope you understand that I have to ask this." He paused, searching for the right words. "Are you and Robert Caldwell personally involved in any way? Or, have you ever been?"

He anxiously watched for her reaction. First, Zoe grimaced, then openly laughed. "Absolutely not," she said. "That was *never, ever* a possibility!"

She took in the puzzled look on Hugh's face and tried to stop herself, though a few more nervous, involuntary giggles escaped before she had herself back under control. She told him, "I guess I need to explain to you why this is so funny."

"The truth is, there are times when I can hardly stand him. Personally, I mean. But in all honesty, he has been pursuing me romantically, for a while now." Her smile faded. "I guess I should start from the beginning, though I don't know if it much matters." She looked inquiringly at Hugh, and he nodded for her to continue.

Zoe's smile faded as she organized her thoughts. Her gaze went past him and out of the window. By the time she turned to face him again, the sadness in her eyes seemed to him like the dark veil of a night without a moon. She told him about her husband's death, and some of the problems that she and Kate were facing. Then, she told him that Robert had begun to pursue her not long after her husband's death, and that Kate was worried about how it would all turn out. In the end, she confessed her intention to quit her job as soon as they returned to Virginia.

It was a long while before she finally ran out of words, and Hugh noted that the effort of the confession had tired her. She was very pale, and there were dark shadows under her eyes. She appeared to Hugh, to be very small and vulnerable.

He reached over and lightly touched her hand. "Zoe, I am really sorry to have had to ask you these questions. I always dislike having to question nice people." He hesitated, then cleared his throat self-consciously and continued, "But, I've especially hated having to do it this time."

"Why?" she asked, opening her eyes wide.

"Well," he hesitated, "my gut tells me that you're a really nice person."

She looked at him, and repeated, "Why?" But even as she asked, he saw the growing amusement in her eyes that finally brought a slow smile back to her tired face.

"I apologize for giving you a hard time, Deputy McKenzie, and thank you for the compliment."
With an effort, she roused herself, straightened her posture, and spoke briskly. "Let's just agree to leave it at that."

He answered her bluntly because something in him was unwilling to let it go that easily. "I'm not sure that I want to leave it at that," he answered. "Do you understand what I mean?"

She leaned forward and patted his arm, then quickly withdrew her hand. "Not entirely, but I imagine it's complicated and so it's probably better that we do, all things considered." He wanted to ask what she meant by that, but someone knocked at the door before he could pursue the matter further.

Zoe stood up, but Hugh took her arm and stopped her. "Listen, there might be more that I need to say, even if you don't want to hear it. But, before we can do anything about that, I need to ask you to do something that will help with this investigation, if you're willing."

She frowned and nodded. He abruptly let go of her arm and she moved to the door and swung it open. Outside, stood Kate, Woolf, Sarah, and a man that she could only assume was Sarah's elusive step-father. He was a solidly-built man of medium-height, with broad shoulders and an overall appearance of brute-strength. His dirty-blond hair was combed straight back, and his cold, blue eyes, so different from Hugh's, shrewdly appraised her before he finally grinned and introduced himself. His smile did not reach his eyes.

"Hey," the man said, "I'm glad to finally meet you. I'm Steve Miller, and I understand that you've been really good to Sarah, here." He gestured toward the girl who stood quietly between himself and Kate. Without waiting for a response, he continued. "I also understand from the girls that you're having some trouble here. That you've actually been threatened by someone."

She opened her mouth to answer, but he interrupted and continued, instead. "Now, before you tell me that this is none of my business, just let me say that if you were my wife or sister," he looked her up and down as though considering either possibility, "I'd tell you to just pack up and leave."

Hugh had reached Zoe's side by the time she had opened the door, and he now stood protectively beside her with his arms folded. Steve, of course, knew who he was, but neither of the men acknowledged the other.

Steve continued, "You seem like nice people and we don't want anything to happen to you, do we Hugh?" He finally acknowledged the deputy and looked directly at him, but Hugh betrayed nothing except his wariness. In fact, the tension between the two men was almost palpable, and Zoe guessed that whatever the reason for it might be, that tension had existed for a very long time.

She answered first. "Thank you, Steve. I appreciate your advice. In fact, Deputy McKenzie was just talking to me about that," she lied. "And, I'm trying to decide how to work everything out in the best way, possible. By the way," she added, nodding at Sarah, "you have a really great girl, there. Thanks for sharing her with us."

"Yeah, well," he shuffled closer to Zoe and stood directly in front of her, close enough to make her take an involuntary step backward. "I've told her that she can stay here again tonight, since you've invited her. But meanwhile, think about what I said, okay?" He glanced at Hugh again, and refreshed his artificial smile.

"These are nice folks, Hugh," he persisted. "Tell her that I'm right. Who knows what kind of nut-case is on the loose out here. Frankly, I'm putting an alarm-system on my own house. I've been thinking about it anyway, what with Sarah being alone there, sometimes."

"That sounds like a very good idea," Zoe agreed. "Maybe Graham Owen will do the same after I tell him about this."

Steve didn't comment on that. Instead, he was suddenly in a hurry to leave. "Okay," he said, "I'm going to head back home now, but if anything else happens, call me and I'll be glad to help out." He pointed at Sarah. "She'll give you my cell number." Steve turned away from the door and Hugh finally spoke in a strained voice.

"Goodnight, Steve; I'll be seeing you around." The other man nodded and left.

Once the door was shut and locked, Kate looked questioningly at her mother, then at Hugh. She clearly intended to say something, but changed her mind. Maybe because of Sarah. However, Zoe acted as though she hadn't noticed. Instead, she put her arms around both girls and gently guided them towards the stairs. She would try to get Kate alone later and find out what was on her mind.

"Baths first, girls, then dinner, and maybe a movie. After all, we need to try out that DVD player while we're here."

The girls reluctantly climbed the stairs. Kate paused and looked back, and her mother nodded, so she went on. She knew that they would talk later, after Hugh had gone and Sarah was sleeping.

As soon as she heard the upstairs bathroom door loudly shut, Zoe turned to Hugh. "What was that all about? I take it that you and Steve Miller are not friends?" Her eyes still looked tired, but she flashed an amused grin at him.

Hugh chuckled, but also made no attempt to hide his irritation. "Not in this lifetime," he snapped. Zoe raised her eyebrows.

"Alright," he sighed. "If you must know, we've been acquainted with each other for quite a few years now, and the guy is a jerk. In fact, I'd bet good money that he wouldn't know the meaning of the term 'legal' if it slapped him in the face and introduced itself to him."

Her lips quivered, but she managed not to laugh. "You do have a way with words, Deputy McKenzie. So, you two have had a few run-ins in the past?"

He chuckled at his own words, and then sighed. "You might say that. Though mostly, it's the attitude that I get from him whenever we run into each other. He's too smart to try much else, though; just a lot of arrogant attitude."

Chapter Seventeen

Late that night, long after Zoe, Kate, and Sarah had gone to sleep, they were all rudely awakened by the sound of one loud crash, soon followed by a succession of additional crashes. The floors and walls shook with each explosion of sound. Zoe leaped from her bed and ran downstairs. She went to the kitchen where Woolf was wildly barking, and then realized that the sounds were coming from underneath the house. Someone must have been beating the floor joists above, with a heavy object. She was disoriented by the noise, and also by the fact that she'd just woken up, so that she could hardly think what to do next.

As it turned out, the decision was made for her by Kate and Sarah, who both flew through the kitchen door with Kate leading as usual. They skidded to a halt in front of her and attempted to shout over the noise. But, instead of shouting back at them, Zoe put her finger to her lips and motioned for the girls to be quiet.

"Stay here and don't make another sound," she whispered. "Whoever it is can probably only hear Woolf, but let's not take any chances. We don't want them to know where we are right now."

The girls, eyes large with fright, scooted into the corner farthest away from the sound and huddled together while Zoe tiptoed from one window to the next, through each of the rooms, trying to catch a glimpse of who the noisemaker might be. Finally, the ear-shattering sounds abruptly stopped and she glimpsed a shadowy figure running away from the front of the house. Whoever it was, was wearing dark clothing. Woolf suddenly lunged at the door and barked wildly. But, when she didn't let him out, his rage diminished and was expressed in intermittent growls, while everyone else breathed a little more easily.

"Mom, you need to call Hugh," Kate begged, tugging at the sleeve of her mother's robe. "He said to call him if anything happened." She was clearly scared, and rightly so. She quickly brushed her hand across her eyes where a few tears had gathered, and was ashamed of them. After all, she needed to be able to help her mother take care of things, now.

But, to Kate's surprise, Zoe shook her head. "No, Kate. Because whoever it was, will be long-gone before Hugh could ever get dressed and over here. We are all fine, and there doesn't appear to be any real damage done to the house, so there is no point in waking him up." She looked at her daughter's anxious face and relented. "I'll call him first-thing in the morning," she added.

"Okay, girls," she motioned them towards the stairway, "Let's go back upstairs. I'm going to call Robert in the morning, too, to see what he might know about this. Meanwhile though, let's go back to bed. Woolf will take good care of us, don't worry," she firmly stated, though she didn't feel nearly as confident as she hoped she appeared to be. In fact, at that moment, she was pretty much convinced that they should just pack up and leave in the morning, at the first light of dawn. Whatever was going on in this house was not their problem, nor did she want it to be.

Instead of heading for her own room, Kate followed her mother into her bedroom. "Mom, what are you going to call Robert for? I mean, he can't help us," she anxiously reasoned.

"No, Kate, I'm not going to ask for his help." She gently brushed a strand of Kate's hair back from her eyes. "I just want to see if he knows any good reason why someone might want us out of this house." Kate didn't' answer, and Zoe gathered her daughter into her arms and held her close.

"Just trust me, Honey. I really don't want his help; I just want to see what he knows, or if he knows, anything about this. And, remember what I told you a couple of days ago—we won't be seeing too much more of him, in any case." Kate sighed and leaned against her mother.

"Okay," she whispered.

Chapter Eighteen

True to her word, Zoe called Hugh first-thing in the morning, and he rushed over, angry that she hadn't called him during the night while the incident was actually taking place.

"For heaven's sake, Zoe," his voice rose, "I might have been able to see who it was or to even have followed him!"

Zoe slid a cup of hot coffee across the table at him as she defended herself. "It didn't last that long. By the time you'd have got dressed and over here, he, or she, would have been long-gone, anyway."

"By the way," she added, "my money is on a 'he' because whatever they used to pound the floor with sounded really heavy, like it would have required some strength to wield." She pulled out the chair opposite Hugh's and sat down. She pushed away her empty cup, rested her elbows on the table, and cupped her chin in her hands.

"You must be really tired," Hugh looked at her closely. "I know this is all an awful strain and I hate that you are going through this, whatever it is." He impulsively leaned across and patted her arm as he spoke. His hand lingered and she slowly withdrew her arm and sat up straight. She also changed the subject.

"I have decided to call Robert this morning, to try to find out what he knows, or doesn't know."

Hugh also sat up straight. "Do you really think that's a good idea? Look, if he's in on whatever this is, he might pick up that you suspect him of being involved in some way and then, you'll really be in danger."

Zoe didn't answer, but he observed the quick defiance in her eyes and the sudden set of her jaw, and he knew that no matter what he said, she was going to telephone Robert, anyway.

He sighed. "Okay, I give up. But, you be really, really careful about what you say and how you say it." Hugh finished the rest of his coffee, stood up, pushed in his chair, and headed for the door. "Call me later and let me know what he says," he said.

An hour later, after Zoe had the two girls completing their home-school assignments up in Kate's room, she shut the downstairs office door and rang Robert's work number. His voice-mail picked up and she breathed a sigh of relief. Her heart was pounding hard, because, in spite of her efforts, she still had no good idea about the best way to approach him. She admitted to herself that she was just hoping that, once he answered, an opening would present itself. She also admitted to herself that that was a pretty weak-kneed approach, but she was afraid that he might be able to pick up the fact that she suspected him in some way. Meanwhile, she would focus on the end of the collections book.

Not long after, her cell phone rang and she involuntarily jumped. She looked at the number and panicked; it was Robert returning her call. She hadn't left a message and still had no good idea about what to say to him.

"Darn, darn, darn!" she exclaimed aloud, and more softly added, "Okay, get a grip. Breathe and try to act natural." She answered the phone in what she hoped was a normal manner.

"Hi, Zoe," he began. "I see that you called. How is everything there? I've been expecting you to at least give me an update about the book. How's it coming?" he asked.

"Hi, Robert," she coolly answered. "The book is nearly finished. I have been working on it, though we've been enjoying the beach, too. You know how it is. But, I am working on it even as we speak, and should easily be able to meet the publishing deadline for you."

They both paused, waiting for the other to speak. Then Robert repeated, "How is everything there?" She drew a deep breath and hoped for the best. "It's great here; we love it." She waited a moment but he said nothing, so she continued.

"We have had a little excitement here, but just kids' pranks, we think."

Robert sharply asked, "What kind of excitement? And, what makes you think that kids were behind it?"

She forced a laugh, but the sound caught in her throat. "Oh, someone knocking on the windows and then on the floor of the house. Nothing too serious, you know. Just kid stuff."

"I don't know, Zoe," he continued. "You're staying in a pretty isolated place. I mean, this has to be making you kind of nervous, doesn't it?"

"Not really," she lied. "We're okay—Woolf takes good care of us." She plunged ahead, for better or for worse. "Also, we've met a local deputy here, and he's looking out for us. So, there's really nothing much to worry about, as you can see. "

She heard him draw in a quick breath. "You know there isn't anything I wouldn't do for you and Kate, don't you?" He waited for her answer, but Zoe said nothing, so he continued.

"Well then, take my advice and just pack up and come home. I need to know that you're safe, that's all. And, if you still feel like you need to get away, we'll make other arrangements for you. How do you feel about the Shenandoah Valley? I have some friends who have a house in Nelson County..." his words trailed off, uncertainly.

"No, thanks, "Zoe firmly replied. "We're okay here. We're just going to stay so don't worry about us, I'm sure that everything is fine."

"But," he began, and she cut him off by plunging into a detailed account of the work that she had completed, and the changes that she intended to make to the book. His responses were vague, as though he had no interest, and she thought that perhaps he was, instead, focused on what might be the best way to persuade her to change her mind. Then again, she thought, perhaps he was simply busy working on his computer while she rambled on. Either way, the conversation obviously wasn't accomplishing anything, so she decided to end it.

"Okay, well, I'll let you get back to work, Robert, and will call you again in a few days...," she began, but he interrupted her.

"Just come back home, Zoe," he insisted. "I need you here in the office for now, and I promise that I'll let you take a couple of weeks off again, as soon as the book is finished. Just pack up and come home."

"But, Robert..." she argued.

His temper snapped for no reason that was apparent to her, and the sternness of his voice surprised her. "That's final, Zoe. No argument. Come back now," he said. "Don't forget that you work for me, and that's an order."

"On the other hand," her anger flared, "working for you isn't synonymous with being owned by you. So, I'll see you whenever I decide to come back!"

She moved her finger to end the call and heard him shout, "Don't, Zoe! Don't you dare hang up!" But, she hung up anyway.

Chapter Nineteen

Other than a few more futile attempts made by Robert to reach Zoe on her cell phone, the rest of the day passed quietly. By late afternoon, she had convinced herself that they had, all of them, simply over-reacted to a prank and nothing more. A nasty prank, she conceded, but a prank, nonetheless. She wondered if she should return Robert's call, but decided not to. She planned to leave the museum for good before long, anyway. And besides, now that she'd had time to consider the possibility, she could quite easily believe him capable of being mixed up in something illegal. "No," she decided. It would be best to distance herself from him in every way, from now on.

As she sliced tomatoes and avocadoes for a salad, Zoe reflected that she had accomplished a lot of work since morning. It wouldn't take long now to wrap up the collections book, and then she and Kate could cut their visit short and go home. But, there was also the matter of Sarah, who wasn't really her responsibility. Actually, there was nothing much she could do about Sarah. After all, she had no proof of any actual mistreatment, or even that Steve left Sarah alone regularly. Maybe it was only once in a great while. Besides which, she and Kate had to leave in another week and a half anyway, at the latest, and probably much sooner than that, the way things were going.

And, what about the threat painted on the front of the house? Zoe stirred the New England clam chowder she'd assembled, and left it simmering while she went into the darkening living room to turn on a light. First though, she pulled a curtain back and watched as the first, pale stars grew brighter above the coral glow of the deepening sunset. She was certain that there would be frost tonight, and she unconsciously pulled her sweater more tightly around herself.

Fortunately, the rest of the night passed quietly. By morning, Zoe was confident that they really had over-reacted to nothing more than a prank. In fact, she decided to celebrate by taking the girls to visit the town of Manteo. Maybe they would even go to the North Carolina Aquarium, located nearby.

The girls were excited about their day-trip, but as they grabbed their jackets and passed through the open front door, Kate stopped abruptly. "Hey, Mom, what about Woolf? Does he still have to stay here and guard the house?"

Zoe looked around at Woolf, who anxiously sat by the front door. His dark eyes pleaded with her, as only a dog's eyes can do. Zoe considered him for a moment, and then relented.

"Come on, boy," she said, and then explained to the girls. "I know that Hugh told us to leave him here, but I really think everything is fine for now. And besides, he's used to going pretty much everywhere with us. I don't like to leave him." Having said that, she double-checked that the locks were secure on both doors, while Woolf ran in excited circles around her feet.

"I've never seen a dog do that," Sarah giggled. "But, I haven't been around many dogs, either."

Kate grinned. "He's just an over-grown puppy when he gets excited, like you're seeing now." Both girls climbed into the backseat and scooted over to make room for Woolf, but Zoe put him in the front passenger seat, instead.

"You'll be a little crowded with him back there," she explained. "And, maybe you'd each like a window-seat without Woolf competing for one, too."

Chapter Twenty

The day passed quietly and pleasantly, as did the following three days. In the meantime, much to Hugh's relief, Zoe's background report verified that she had no criminal record, and also revealed that what she'd told him about herself was true. Hugh wasn't really surprised, but at the same time, felt that a weight had been lifted off his shoulders. She was exactly what she said she was, and now he could focus his attention on what had happened and what might happen next.

He wasn't convinced that the worst was over, though he hadn't heard anymore from her, so he presumed that all was well, at least for the moment. He pulled out his personal cell phone and ruefully smiled to himself because he had put her number on speed-dial. And, he promised himself that he would never admit that to anyone else, including her.

Meanwhile, Zoe chose to believe that they had seen the last of any trouble, though the girls were not entirely convinced, and remained cautious.

"Sometimes, she just believes what she wants to believe," Kate remarked to Sarah one evening while they were up in Kate's bedroom playing the board-game, *Clue*, that they had found in a cupboard. Sarah shrugged.

"I s'pose it's better than being scared all the time," she observed. "Maybe pretending that something is true will make it true."

Kate shook her head, stretched out her legs, and leaned on one elbow. "I don't see how it could. I think we still need to be careful because we don't know who did this stuff, or why."

Later that afternoon, the doorbell rang. Woolf growled as he followed Zoe to the door, where she hesitated, then called out, "Who is it?"

A deep voice answered, "It's Graham Owens. I don't know if you're aware of this, but I own this house and heard from Deputy McKenzie that there have been some problems here. Can I please come in and talk to you?"

Zoe hesitated. "Do you have some sort of personal identification with you, Mr. Owens? My German shepherd is standing here beside me, and I promise that I will set him loose on you if you aren't who you say you are," she threatened. "Furthermore, I'm calling Deputy McKenzie right now to tell him that you're here," she added.

Fortunately, Hugh answered his cell phone right away. Zoe was clearly upset; he heard it in her voice. "Hugh, wherever you are, please get over here right away. There's a man at the door who claims to be Graham Owen. And if he's not, there's a problem. And if he is, then he may be in on whatever is going on out here, and that's a problem, too."

"Hey, I'm at home, so I'll be there in about two minutes," he assured her. "Don't open the door until I get there." But, as he ran toward the house, he could see that she hadn't waited for him. Instead, she was standing in the open doorway with Woolf, whose teeth were bared. Needless to say, Graham Owens, if that's who he really was, wasn't making any move to cross the threshold, and Hugh sincerely hoped that Woolf wouldn't attack until they could at least verify his identification.

"I'm here," he called, breathing heavily, as he ran up the steps. Without further conversation, the frustrated stranger thrust his driver's license at him.

"Here," he said, between clenched teeth. "Look at it. I am Graham Owens and you called me a few days ago about some trouble, here. I decided that I'd better make the trip down, and find out for myself what is going on." He glared at them both and added, "After all, this is my house, and I have a right to know about anything that happens, here."

"You're absolutely right, Mr. Owens," Hugh said, as he motioned them both back inside the house.

Graham Owens pushed his way past Hugh and addressed Zoe from between clenched teeth.

"And remember that *I* didn't rent this house to you, so don't think you can threaten me with your dog. The law is on *my* side in this. I could have you thrown out this minute, if I wanted to."

Zoe bristled, and she returned Graham's angry stare as Hugh quickly stepped in. "That's right, Mr. Owens," he said soothingly as he moved between them, "but you also have to understand that this young woman is frightened for both herself and her daughter, and besides, she believed that she *was* renting the house from you." He waited for more argument, but Graham only frowned, so he continued.

"Let's just all speak civilly to one another and I'll be happy to show you the locked room and explain everything that we know, so far. Does that work for you, Mr. Owens?

Graham Owens took a deep breath and released it. "Okay," he nodded in Woolf's direction. "But keep that dog away from me."

Chapter Twenty-One

A few minutes later, after examining the combination lock on the bedroom door, Graham took a seat in the rocking chair downstairs and warily eyed Woolf, who continued to closely watch him, as well, from where he sat, close against Zoe's feet. She had seated herself at the far end of the couch, as though intending to stay as far away from Graham as possible.

Hugh sat down in one of the arm-chairs, and gave her a warning glance in the hope that she would understand his need to handle the situation without interference from her. Her eyes were still defiant, but she had clearly understood, and Hugh only hoped that the truce would last. He leaned forward, gripping the arms of his comfortable chair, as he turned to face Graham.

"First of all, Mr. Owens, how long have you known Robert Caldwell?

With his attention distracted away from Zoe and Woolf, Graham relaxed against the back of his chair, and thought for a moment. "Let's see...about five years, I'd say. We met at a museum conference in Washington, where I live," he added, "and we've run across each other often, since then. He's a really nice guy, as far as I know."

Graham absently smoothed the front of his jacket and continued. "Robert is one of those highly-stressed people. In fact," he smiled wistfully, "he's one of those people who also seems to share his stress with everyone around him. Sometimes, that makes him difficult to want to be around, and I've always felt kind of sorry for him. I thought that maybe, if he could get away and come here once in a while, it might help him unwind. So, I gave him a key and told him to use the house when he wanted, but, of course, to also check with me first whenever he planned to come down. I honestly thought that I could trust him."

He sat up abruptly and looked at Zoe. "But you work for him, don't you? Do you see him as being that way, too?"

She nodded and pursed her lips. "Yes. I would have assumed I could trust him, too. And regarding his stress, well, I agree that his stress is everybody's stress. And generally, everything needs to be his way. He doesn't take suggestions from anyone very well."

"I've suspected that," Graham chuckled. Before he could pursue that line of thought though, Hugh changed the direction of the conversation.

"What do you know about Robert Caldwell as a private collector?"

"Nothing much," Graham shook his head. "Why?"

"It's just a line of inquiry that we're following," Hugh explained. "We think that his interests might have something to do with whatever is going on, here."

"Oh, Lord," Graham moaned and covered his face with his hands, then lowered them again. "Why did I ever trust him? I'll never do such a stupid thing, again, as long as I live."

"I understand, sir," said Hugh. "But, back to the question, what do you know?"

"Not much," he answered. "I know that he likes the really ancient stuff, because once in a while he has mentioned some things that he'd picked up at auctions and from private dealers. But, that's about it, you know. It's not like we've spent a lot of time together. Or, that I have actually seen any of the stuff he's collected," he added.

Graham turned his head and looked pleadingly at Zoe. "I honestly thought that he was just a nice guy who needed to get away sometimes; that's really all I know. You know him better than I do, I'm sure."

She nodded, her eyes sympathetic at his obvious distress. "Yes, I agree with what you say about him, and I do believe that you were just trying to be nice to him. I've always thought of him as the type of person who looks for other people to help him. And," she added," he has, in this case, obviously taken advantage of your kindness."

Graham offered her a hint of a smile and nodded his appreciation before turning to Hugh. "So, tell me everything."

Hugh proceeded to explain everything that had happened so far, and then, with a quick glance at Zoe, turned their attention back to the problem of the locked door. "Let's go back upstairs and see if we can figure out a way to get into that room without breaking down the door," he proposed.

But, to his surprise, Graham said, "If you need to break it down, just do it."

"I'd rather not do that, just now" Hugh explained. "Whatever is in there, we need to know who put it there and who it belongs to, and we're just speculating about Robert. We have no proof that he is involved, and besides, we also need to know who else might be in on this. So, if we are able to get inside, we also need to be able to get back out and leave it just as it looks, right now."

Both men rose and climbed the stairs to see what might be done about unlocking the door without appearing to have done so. No sooner were they out of sight, than Kate and Sarah rushed into the house through the back door, and slammed it behind themselves.

"Hey, Mom!" Kate called. "Where are you?" But when Zoe entered the kitchen, Kate abruptly stopped talking. She had noticed the expression on her mother's face, and sensed that something important had taken place while the two of them had been outdoors.

"Girls," Zoe addressed them both, "the man who owns this house is here. He and Hugh are upstairs right now, looking around. So, while they're doing that, we are going to just stay here in the kitchen and not distract them."

"Did something else happen?" Kate's eyes were anxious.

"No," Zoe reassured her. "Everything is still fine, but Mr. Owens is understandably upset about his house being vandalized." She waved her arm toward the stove. "Come on now; while they're looking around, let's make ourselves something to eat."

No one was hungry at that moment, but Zoe couldn't think of any other way to keep them in the kitchen, indefinitely. "Let's make S'mores," she offered. S'mores would not take long to make and even less time to eat, yet they seemed as good as any solution for passing the time. Zoe knew that as long as the girls were absorbed with their project, they would be content. And, they could ask her questions and voice their opinions, later.

The three of them were sitting at the kitchen table, helping themselves from a plateful, when the men returned. Zoe told the men to help themselves, and also offered to make coffee for them, but neither wanted any. "No luck," Hugh informed her," but it was worth a try."

Graham pulled out a chair and sat down heavily, as though his legs wouldn't support him any longer. He rubbed a hand distractedly across his forehead. "I can't imagine why Robert would lock that room. You really do think that he's the one who did that, don't you? "

"Honestly, if no one else has a key to this house, who else could have done it?" Hugh shrugged. "Is it possible that someone else might have had your key copied?" Graham shook his head.

"No, I'm really careful about such things. But, of course, Robert could have copied it for someone else," he admitted.

Hugh's voice was gentle as he abruptly changed the subject. "What do you plan to do now, Graham? Are you heading back to Washington today?"

The distraught man shook his head. "I think I should stick around here for a couple of days, anyway." He looked up at Zoe. "In a hotel, you understand; I'm not trying to stay here at the house with you."

In spite of herself, Zoe felt sorry for him. He was clearly, very upset. "There is an extra, unoccupied bedroom here, and you're certainly welcome to stay with us, if you'd like to," she offered. "After all, this is your own house. You can have your meals here with us, too."

"But, on the other hand, we will pack up and leave, if you'd like us to do so."

He smiled wanly at her, though the worried look in his eyes never wavered. "I'm already booked in at a hotel, but thanks anyway. Really," he spoke emphatically, "I do appreciate the offer." His gaze wandered over the room as though he was memorizing it.

"I haven't been here in quite a while," he said, "but there's no reason for you to leave if you want to stay."

Hugh rose and clapped a hand on Graham's shoulder. "We're closely watching the house, I promise you. And, I'll let you know right away if anything else happens."

Graham took the hint, got up, and slung his expensive, down-jacket loosely over his shoulder.

"Thanks," he nodded. "I'm at the Hampton Inn if you need me. I'll be working from there, but I'm around." He caught Zoe's eye. "You know how it is in this business; it never stops," he smiled again.

Hugh and Zoe both walked Graham to where his SUV was parked in the driveway. While the two men exchanged cell numbers, Zoe noticed Susan Hall trudging toward them through the sand.

"Great," she murmured, as she squared her shoulders. "That's just what we need, right now."

Hugh and Graham were still talking, and hadn't noticed the older woman approaching. When she reached the end of the short driveway, she hurried toward them.

"Hello, Graham!" she called. "I saw your car and wanted to say hello! After all, it's been a long time since we've chatted."

Her eyes were bright with excitement. "Have you heard that the Ghost Horse is back? Several people have seen him, you know. And, best of all, he's been seen at the edge of the shore just opposite this house. Isn't that wonderful?" She beamed as she took hold of his arm.

Graham visibly blanched. "What on earth are you talking about?" His voice suddenly trembled as though he was close to reaching his breaking point. He shook off Susan's iron-clawed grip and slipped into the front seat, slammed the door, started the engine and shifted the car into reverse.

Hugh grabbed Susan Hall and pulled her out of the way as Graham Owens floored the engine and spun both sand and gravel, in all directions.

Hugh watched in amazement. "If he keeps that up, he won't be going anywhere." He shook his head. "Surely the fool knows that you can't drive like that out here." In the next breath, he asked, "Are you alright, Ms. Hall?"

"Yes, dear," she replied, seemingly not at all disturbed by Graham's rudeness. "He must be in an awful hurry." She brushed sand off her jacket.

"Oh, well, Graham is a busy man and he probably doesn't understand about the horse," she reasoned. "And, I'm sure that he thinks I'm just a foolish old woman, but that's alright. He'll learn," she looked up, hopefully. "Don't you agree?"

Zoe didn't trust herself to speak. She avoided looking at Susan Hall, and focused on the ground, instead. Her sympathy was completely for Graham Owens, who had undoubtedly dealt with her, before.

But Hugh was a compassionate man, and he answered kindly. "That's so, Ms. Hall; he'll learn one of these days."

He glanced over at Zoe as he patted the older woman's shoulder. "We have to go now, Ms. Hall, but I'm sure we'll see you later." He put his other hand on Zoe's back and guided her toward the house.

"Good-bye!" Susan called. "Remember to keep an eye out for the horse and everything will turn out just fine!"

At that, Zoe whipped around and angrily stared at the old woman. But Hugh's hand firmly pushed her up the steps and into the house, instead. Once he'd shut the door, he turned to face her.

"Leave it, okay? She's just an old woman, and I've known her long enough to know that she doesn't mean any harm to anyone. If seeing that horse makes her feel better, then so what?" he asked.

"Besides, what are you so angry about? How can this poor woman possibly bother you, at all?"

Zoe's voice rose. "What do you mean 'if seeing that horse...'" she began, but then redirected the subject. "Never mind. She—and that horse—are the least of my problems!" Zoe took a deep breath and in a calmer voice, asked, "So, what do we do now?"

She had abruptly changed the subject because Hugh's comments stung, not least because he was right. Why, exactly was she so angry with Susan? No immediate, good answer came to her. "I'll think about it later," she promised herself.

"Nothing," Hugh abruptly answered her question. He leaned his back against the closed door. "We now know that whatever is going on, Graham Owens isn't in on it. Believe me, I've been in this line of work long enough to know when someone is lying to me, and he wasn't lying. He doesn't know anything and he's scared. And, rightly so," he added.

"Someone is using the man's house for some sort of illegal activity, and we just have to figure out the rest of it. I want him out of the way though, for now. I need to be able to control this investigation without outside interference. By the way," he added, "What did you think of him?"

Zoe shrugged. "Nothing much. He's high-strung, but probably a decent person. Why?"

"I felt sorry for him," Hugh grinned, "but I also thought he was pretty full of himself. A tad pompous, I guess you'd say."

Zoe returned his grin and folded her arms. "Yeah? Well, welcome to my world."

Hugh chuckled, but a moment later, his eyes narrowed and his tone grew serious. "I have an idea," was all he would say. "I have to go now; I'll be in touch with you a little later."

Zoe was relieved to close and lock the door behind him. She very much wanted some time to herself, and perhaps a cup of hot tea, as well. She headed for the kitchen.

Chapter Twenty-Two

Later that same night, Sarah slept soundly while Kate woke up feeling restless. Ever since she'd first seen what she believed was the Ghost Horse, she'd been closely watching the shore, though she certainly wasn't' going to admit that to either Sarah or to her mother. Sarah meant well, but she might accidentally say something and Kate didn't want to stir up another argument.

As much as she might disagree with Zoe, Kate also knew that there was no point in trying to discuss it with her. She sighed as a sense of loneliness swept over her. Since her dad's death, she often felt isolated and lonely. But, she didn't dare tell her mother that, either.

Still unable to sleep, Kate got up and went to stare out of the window, as usual. Silvery-gray clouds wafted across the growing moon. All seemed quiet outside, except for the ever-blowing wind, and Kate could see no movement except that of the clouds. After a while, she gave up and decided to go back to bed. But, as she turned to go, something caught her eye. A shadowy light moved along the shore, as though someone might be trying to subdue the brightness of their flashlight. She watched for a moment and saw that there were two people. Maybe they were just taking a late-night walk along the shore. But then, just as she decided once again to give it up and go back to bed, her breath caught in her throat.

The people and their flashlight had disappeared, but just opposite the house, a white horse stood at the edge of the shore. She was sure of it, this time. A very faint glow surrounded it, and Kate wondered if the glow was a reflection from the moonlight. Then again, maybe not; maybe the light was actually coming from the horse. She couldn't be sure. From the top of the dresser, she snatched up the binoculars that had been her dad's last birthday gift to her, and rushed back to the window. But, the horse had already gone. Frustrated, she couldn't quite stifle a groan. She knew that she would only continue to question herself. Had she really seen a horse? Or, had she just seen it because she wanted to see it?

Kate pressed her lips into a thin line and made her decision. Of course she'd seen it. And no one, including her mother, was going to convince her, otherwise. As usual, she just wouldn't tell anyone, but somehow, simply seeing the horse and affirming that she'd seen him, made her feel better. Made her feel safer.

Not long after, she fell asleep and, toward morning, dreamed about her father. He called her name, and she desperately tried to find him in spite of being surrounded by thick, impenetrable fog. In the dream, she stumbled along what seemed to be the sea-shore and kept calling out to him, but she couldn't see him, anywhere.

Then, suddenly and unaccountably, she was lying in her own bed, in her own room, in the house at the beach. She believed that she was completely awake at this point, and found herself sitting up, propped against her pillows. She looked carefully around the dimly, moonlit room and gasped as her eyes focused on her father, who was standing at the foot of her bed, looking at her. She pulled herself up straighter so that she could see him better. At the same time, somewhere in the back of her mind, she wondered where Woolf was. He would be wild with joy to see him, again. But then, she saw that Woolf was curled up beside her bed, as usual, and was sound asleep. And so, in that moment, Kate knew that only she, alone, had the ability to see him.

There were no surprises; he looked exactly as he had always done. He had no visible wounds, at least as far as she could see, and he still wore his military uniform. In his hand, he held a small, pinkish-tinged clam shell, such as one commonly found on the Corolla beaches. She held out her hand to him and whispered, "Daddy?" He did not answer, but instead, held a warning finger to his lips, prompting her to be quiet. Then, he smiled.

Chapter Twenty-Three

The next thing Kate knew, she was waking up to bright sunlight with no thought other than that of what her mother might cook for breakfast. She stretched comfortably and noticed that Woolf was no longer beside her bed. The sun was high, so she knew she'd slept later than usual. She threw a quick glance in the direction of Sarah's bed, but it was empty. Sarah had already gone downstairs and Woolf must have followed her.

With a yawn, Kate threw her covers back and snatched up her hair brush from the dresser. She stood in front of the mirror inspecting her own, sleep-tousled appearance. But then, something else caught her attention and she caught her breath. In the mirror's reflection, she saw a small, pink clam shell lying at the foot of her bed. And, the memory of her strange dream swept over her with the cold shock of ice water. She even shivered as a faint gust of cold wind blew over her and the hair on the back of her neck stood up. But, she noted, the windows were closed.

Not stopping to ponder the unexpected breeze, Kate snatched up the shell, opened her top-right dresser drawer, and thrust it inside, under her socks. She needed time to think. Her father must have actually come to her in the night, and had left the shell as a reminder. But, of course, she could never tell her mother what had happened. The shell, itself, was common enough on that beach, and she feared that her mother might just toss it back outside if she came in to straighten the room later.

Kate hardly noticed which clothes she picked up and threw on. It didn't matter, anyway. All she could think about was her father's visit and the Ghost Horse. She shivered. Seeing both of them had to mean that something was wrong. Something was going to happen. Above all, she needed to figure out exactly what that meant, so that she could protect both her mother and herself. Or, was Sarah the one facing trouble? Sarah had been with them each time the horse had appeared. But surely her own father wouldn't have come to her if Sarah was the one who was in danger.

She gritted her teeth in frustration. She needed time to think. She had to figure this out, for all their sakes. But, would she be able to do that in time? Kate grabbed her shoes and ran down the steps, two-at-a-time. She was forced to slow down when she reached the slippery, hard-wood floor at the bottom, but still hurried into the kitchen as fast as she could manage. She found Sarah there, sitting at the table and eating a bowl of cold cereal.

Sarah paused with her spoon in mid-air. "What's the hurry? Is something wrong?"

Woolf got up and trotted over to her. Kate reached down and gently ran her hand over his shiny coat. "No, I'm just in a hurry to get down to the shore," she replied. "Are you almost finished?"

Zoe entered, just in time to hear Kate's explanation, and insisted that she sit down to eat something before going anywhere. Kate huffed and rolled her eyes, but opened the bread-bag and put a slice in the toaster. "At least toast is portable," she thought to herself. She was no longer hungry, at all.

"Since Sarah's already finished, I can just take the toast with me, can't I?" she begged.

Zoe yawned and removed a coffee mug from the shelf. "I suppose so, this time," she acquiesced.

Sarah finished up and put her bowl and spoon in the dishwasher, then the girls each grabbed their jackets and rushed outside. The first thing Kate did was to examine the sand for hoof-prints, but she saw none. She was hoping for some sort of supernatural sign; maybe one would turn up soon, anyway.

Kate also fervently hoped that her mother would not look too closely into her sock-drawer. She needed to come up with a better place to hide that shell. Someplace where she could also safely retrieve it without anyone noticing. She shook her blowing hair away from her face. She was tired and anxious, and had absolutely no idea what was going on.

As the girls walked, Kate wordlessly went over, in her mind, the events of the previous night. If only she could ask someone's advice. But, there was no one. Maybe she would try to research symbolic meanings on the computer later, if she could maneuver enough privacy to do so. Neither Zoe nor Sarah could know about it, though, and that might be a problem.

As it turned out, the girls didn't stay outside very long. The wind was cold and darkening clouds moved quickly over the dimming face of what had changed into a pale, morning sun. They had just agreed to return to the house when Sarah noticed something partially buried in the sand close to her foot. She bent down, carefully retrieved a small, gold coin, and held it in the palm of her hand to show to Kate.

"I've never seen anything like this. What do you think it is?" she asked, turning it over.

Kate shrugged. "I've never seen anything like that either. Bring it along and we'll show it to Mom. Maybe she'll know." She shielded her eyes and looked up at the sky. She was not interested in the coin; she had far more important things to think about.

"It's freezing out here. We can come back later. Who knows? Maybe we'll find some more of those coins, whatever they are."

"Okay," Sarah readily agreed. She was feeling the cold, too, and paused just long enough to carefully tuck the coin in her jacket pocket.

Meanwhile, Hugh telephoned Zoe, to explain what he had done. "So, I asked Graham Owens to ring Robert from his cell phone and tell him that he was in Corolla, checking on his house. First of all, I want to get Robert's reaction to that," he chuckled. "And, second of all, I want to see if he might just mention where he is, himself, right at the moment."

"Why does his location matter?" Zoe asked. "Why would that be significant?"

Hugh replied patiently, as though explaining to a child. "Because, for all we knew, he isn't really in Virginia at work, and that's important. Now, here's the best part," he continued. Zoe attempted to interrupt him at that point, but he persisted.

"Zoe… it turns out that Robert is not in Virginia, after all. Instead, he's here, in Corolla."

"What do you mean he's in Corolla?" her voice rose. "What exactly does that mean? And, what do we do now?"

"*You* don't do anything," he replied. "And, you must also be careful. For one thing, you certainly don't want to let him into the house where you're staying, for any reason. And, if he should call you, don't answer your phone right away. Let him leave a message and then we'll decide how best to handle it."

He drew a deep breath and continued. "I need to figure out why he's in this area and where he's staying. But, I want you completely out of whatever is going on. Do you understand me? You have to let me make the rules in this situation, and I need you to completely cooperate with me, no matter what. Do you understand?" he repeated.

"Okay," she reluctantly agreed. "So, meanwhile, what am I supposed to tell the girls? That they're not allowed to play outside anymore?"

"I hadn't thought of that," Hugh admitted. "Well, just do the best you can, but whatever happens, don't let him into your house. I don't want him to have access to that locked room, or really, to have access to anywhere else in the house, for that matter. For all we know, he might have staked out another hiding place that we're not yet aware of. You know, like a loose floor board or ceiling tile; something like that."

Chapter Twenty-Four

As soon as Zoe hung up from talking with Hugh, the house telephone rang. She hesitated long enough to check the number, and saw that it was not Robert. But, the number was unfamiliar. She wondered if he might be calling from another phone. But then, she asked herself, why would he? In the end, she decided to take the chance, and was surprised to find that the caller was Steve Miller, Sarah's step-father.

"Hey, is everything okay over there?" his voice was unnecessarily loud. "I thought I saw Graham Owens out front when I drove by, yesterday. But, I haven't seen him anywhere since, and so I thought I'd better check on you. See if you needed any help and just make sure everything is okay."

Zoe held the phone away from her ear and wondered why he was shouting. She would have to think fast. She could hardly deny that Graham had shown up at the house, but at the same time, she didn't dare give away too much information. She cleared her throat.

"Yes, that's right," she said. "The police called him and reported the vandalism to him, and he decided to take a look at the damage, for himself. Just to be able to talk to his insurance company, you know," she added. She thought that sounded like a valid-enough reason for his being there.

Steve paused as though thinking over what she'd said, and then asked, "So, is he staying with you?"

"No." she forced herself to laugh, though it sounded more like she was choking. "He's seen that it's nothing serious and is heading home sometime today, as far as I know." Should she have said that? Well, it was too late now. She would just have to plead ignorance if Steve found out that Graham was actually staying at a local hotel. But, then the thought came to her that Graham might be in personal danger. "Oh dear," she thought. "If that is the case, then he might be safer if people think he is really leaving the area."

Fortunately, Steve seemed to be in a hurry to hang up. "Okay, well, I was just checking to see if everything is fine there. You'll let me know if that changes, okay? I'm just trying to be a good neighbor to you, you know."

Zoe thanked him for his concern and agreed to be in touch if she needed him, in what she hoped was a confident tone of voice. Then, with a huge sense of relief, she hung up. She suddenly felt very tired. She fetched a fresh cup of tea, threw herself onto the couch and tucked her legs up underneath her. "A few minutes is all that I need," she thought. But instead, she suddenly sat bolt-upright.

How would Steve have known the house-phone number? She remembered Robert saying that the number was unlisted, and she couldn't quite imagine that Graham and Steve were friends. On the other hand, perhaps Steve had done some work for Graham in the past. That would explain it.

She pushed the thought aside and leaned back, again. But, her few intended moments of peace evaporated quickly as the girls burst in the back door, clearly excited. She could hear them running through the kitchen.

Sarah reached her first and thrust a small coin into her hand. "Look what I found on the beach, Zoe! Do you know what it is?" Zoe took the coin over to the window where she could see it better, and examined it closely.

"I'm not sure, girls, but this looks really old. I'll tell you what, I'll try to research it on the internet if you'll leave it with me, okay?" She absently patted Sarah's shoulder.

"Hey, Mom," Kate added, "we also found another one just like it right outside the back door. It was right up against the step and if I hadn't had to stop and tie my shoe, we'd have probably never seen it. Isn't that strange?" she added. "Two of the same kind of old coins and one was right outside our door," she marveled.

Zoe reminded herself that she needed to stay calm, in spite of the fact that she had just been presented with yet another mystery that might or might not be related to whatever was already going on. One coin did not seem questionable. Two of them, did. Especially since the second one was close to the house.

"That's pretty cool, girls!" she told them. "It's hard to say how it ended up here with the other one at the shore. Maybe somebody lost them in the sand many years ago, and they have resurfaced. You know how the sand shifts and it's easy to lose things," she vaguely added. She had to think what to do next. And meanwhile, she needed to distract them.

Zoe changed the subject. "Are you two up to mixing up some Rice Krispie treats this morning? If so, you'll find everything you need in the kitchen cupboard to the right of the sink; the upper one, I mean. The recipe is already out on the counter," she added, and waved them toward the kitchen. "I figured you might enjoy making those when you came in from the shore."

The girls shouted, "Yes!" and rushed to the kitchen, and Zoe pushed away thoughts of the mess they would undoubtedly leave behind. She hopefully called, "Remember to butter the pan, and be sure to clean up after yourselves when you're finished!"

A moment later, she sat down at her computer to consider her options. She wanted to finish the collections book by today, and she'd also promised to research Sarah's coin. But, she couldn't help thinking about Robert and Steve, instead. She considered the possibility that she might be over-reacting, where the coins were concerned. It was feasible that the coins had been dropped by someone a very long time ago. At the same time, it did seem odd that if that was the case, they would both surface on the same day.

Had Robert come to the house without her knowing, and accidentally dropped them? That didn't make sense, though. He wouldn't take that kind of chance. And besides, the coins might be valuable. He and Steve both collected coins; maybe Steve had even dropped them when he had come by. It didn't mean that she and Kate were in any danger, she firmly told herself. In fact, there was probably a simple and plausible explanation. She acknowledged though, that she would definitely feel better if she had any idea as to what that plausible explanation might be.

Chapter Twenty-Five

Two hours later, Zoe clicked "Send," on the attachment she was emailing, and the manuscript was on its way to Robert, as well as to the museum's Chairman of the Board of Directors. She had completed the collections book, and she would very soon be free to sever all ties with Robert.

She leaned back in her chair, and considered the future. She would write her letter of resignation sometime today, but she and Kate also needed to decide pretty quickly, where they wanted to live. Wherever that was, it would be far away from Robert. She thought about her sister and wondered if they should move closer to her in New England, after all. Maybe Vermont. They'd always liked the mountains and she and Kate could learn to ski together.

Caught up in day-dreams about the future, Zoe's thoughts eventually drifted back to her husband, and she wondered what he would have thought of their living in New England. She still felt unsure of herself when it came to making major decisions, and she unconsciously tightened her jaw. She would just have to get used to it; there was no alternative. And, hopefully everything would turn out alright for both Kate and herself, in the end.

The girls had long-since finished making and eating their Rice-Krispie treats. In fact, they had managed to eat half of what had been pressed into the pan. They had interrupted her long enough to ask if they could go to Sarah's house for a while. Zoe absent-mindedly agreed, and then Kate asked her if she had found any information about the coin yet, because they wanted to show it to Sarah's step-father. They thought that he might know what it was, just in case Zoe didn't find the information online.

"Sure," she agreed. "Let me just make a quick photocopy of it and I'll see what I can find, and meanwhile, you can take it along to show to your dad."

After they left, Zoe got up and stretched. Now that the book was finished, she would be able to concentrate on finding out what she could about the coin. In a way, she was surprised that the girls had taken the time to pay much attention to it. But, perhaps the fact that it was foreign was a novelty that had attracted them. But, whatever the reason, it probably wasn't important. She began her search, and, nearly an hour later, she located what she was looking for.

It seemed that the coin had originated in ancient Syria. The caption on the online site, described it as from the Armenian Kingdom, Tigranes V (Herodian Tigranes I), c. 6 – 12 A.D.

Zoe propped her elbows on the edge of the desk and cupped her chin in her hands. How would such a coin have found its way to the Outer Banks in North Carolina, and how had it specifically shown up in Corolla? It could be that someone besides Robert and Steve had dropped it. There must be plenty of other collectors. Still, the fact that it came from Syria

concerned her.

She got up to retrieve the sweater she'd left upstairs, but then

stopped abruptly. "What if those coins are actually part of a smuggler's

cache?" she asked herself, aloud. "Or, am I overreacting? Am I seeing

smugglers where there are none? On the other hand, there is Robert, and

there is Steve. And, there is also someone who is trying to frighten us out

of this house," she reminded herself. Or, could it be that Robert and

Steve were the ones trying to frighten her into leaving? After all, Robert

was somewhere in the area, but he had not yet tried to contact her. She

wondered where he was staying.

In the end, she decided to at least call Hugh and tell him about

the coins. He needed to know about them, and also, maybe by now, he

would be able to tell her where Robert was staying. She picked up her cell

phone, but abruptly laid it down again when the doorbell rang.

Chapter Twenty-Six

It was Robert. She could see him through the curtain. Hugh had ordered her not to let him into the house, but her Jeep was parked in the driveway, so obviously, he knew that she was there. She felt panicky, but took a deep breath to calm herself, and considered the best way to handle the situation.

In the end, she decided that there was nothing for it. She had to simply hope for the best, and she threw the door open. The first thing she noticed was that Robert was not radiating his usual, arrogant confidence, but instead, seemed to be agitated.

"Hey, Zoe," he brusquely addressed her. He brushed past her and entered the front hall without waiting for an invitation. By the time she had closed the door, he was already seated in the middle of the large couch in the living room.

"Well, just make yourself at home, Robert." Her smile softened the sarcasm. "To what do I owe this honor? And, why didn't you ring up first and tell me you were coming?"

"I thought I'd surprise you, instead," he explained, as he looked around the room. He seemed to be working hard to avoid directly meeting her eyes.

"Well, what can I do for you?" she asked, and rested her hands on her hips.

"Nothing much; I just need to stay here overnight," was his unexpected reply. "I know you have that extra bedroom and I have some quick business to take care of down this way. And besides, this seemed like a good way to catch up on the news with one another."

Surprise overcame her, and she blustered, "Do we really need to catch up with each other? I haven't been away that long, and was planning to go out with the girls later." The moment she said it, she wished she could have retracted her words. She knew that he would offer to stay in the house while she was gone, and there was no way that she was about to allow that to happen.

And, sure enough, he took her at her word. "That's no problem, Zoe. You go ahead and do whatever you'd planned, and I'll just settle in here while you're gone. I can even cook dinner for us if you'd like," he offered.

"No...that's okay," she attempted to back-pedal. "I can't leave you alone now that you've come all this way. By the way," she breathlessly asked, "what are you doing here? There's no museum business way out here to take care of, is there?"

He finally met her eyes. "Actually, I have been interviewed as a possible consultant for a group in Duck who are interested in starting a local-culture museum. And, as for coming here, I thought I'd combine business with the pleasure of seeing you and Kate again. And, I'm serious about cooking dinner." He rubbed the palms of his hands together, jumped up, and headed for the kitchen. "What have you got to work with?" he asked.

"I am planning to roast a chicken for dinner," she admitted. Meanwhile, her thoughts were spinning. Was it possible to gracefully encourage him to leave? His request seemed perfectly reasonable on the surface, but what if his coming actually had nothing to do with museum business? Unable to come up with any good, workable ideas, Zoe distractedly opened the refrigerator and pulled out the chicken, along with some chopped kale, cranberries, and pecans for a salad.

"By the way, have you had any more problems with vandalism out here?" he casually asked as he opened and closed cupboard doors, looking for whatever might serve as a roasting pan.

"It's been pretty quiet," she said. "Actually, I think it was just a prank; probably some kids with too much time on their hands."

He nodded and told her that he had received her finished collections book and was pleased with it. "I haven't had time to read through it, of course," he explained, "because I've been in that meeting. But, I'm sure it will look good."

He talked on about the book, and his ideas for future publications that they might work on together, and didn't return to the subject of vandalism at all. It all seemed so normal, that she began to wonder if she and Hugh had misjudged him as a possible smuggler.

The girls returned just as Zoe was setting the table. "Where are you, Mom?" Kate shouted as she slammed the back door. She and Sarah removed their sand-laden shoes and danced into the dining area, where they stopped short when they saw Robert.

Zoe did the best she could. "Sarah, I don't think you've met our friend Robert, have you?" Without waiting for a reply, she hurried on. "I work for him, and he's here on business, and is going to spend the night with us, tonight."

Kate raised her eyebrows and mumbled a brief, "Hi" before turning away and brushing an invisible bit of sand from her fleece sweater. Sarah did better. She stepped forward with a shy smile, and Robert chatted with her while Kate went to help her mother bring in the food.

In the kitchen, before Kate could say anything, Zoe stopped her. "He's just here for the night, Kate. There's nothing I can do about that, but it's only for one night," she reasoned. "You and Sarah can watch a movie or play a game; you don't have to interact with him much. But when you do, be polite to him and let's just get through this." Kate nodded. There seemed to be nothing else to say.

During dinner, Robert talked about his plans to visit his parents in Iowa for Christmas, and also kept them entertained with his uncannily accurate, if somewhat unkind, impressions of their co-workers, most of whom Kate also knew. They repeatedly glanced at each other and guiltily giggled. And Sarah, though she didn't know any of the people who being imitated, giggled, as well.

By the time they were rinsing and putting dishes into the dishwasher, Robert was yawning. "Hey, I'm going to turn in early; it's been an extraordinarily busy day for me."

The girls ran off upstairs to play a game and he turned to Zoe and took her hands in his.

"Zoe, when I leave in the morning, I want you and Kate to come with me." She opened her mouth to protest, but he went on. "I mean it; it's not safe here. I should never have brought you to this place. Come on, it's time to just pack it in and go home."

She hesitated. In a way, there was nothing she wanted more than to just give it up and go home. She didn't need or want any more complications in her life. But, on the other hand, what if he really was a smuggler? A crook? Something in her also needed to know the truth about him, one way or the other.

She shook her head. "I can't, Robert. We're going to stay until the end of this week, and then..." her voice trailed off.

"No—I insist that you come with me, Zoe." He said. "I mean it. If you won't pack your bags, I'll pack them for you, but you're leaving with me in the morning, like it or not."

If he hadn't added that last bit, Zoe might have given in. But no one enjoys being ordered about, and she was no different. Her green eyes flashed. "Stop it, Robert," her voice was deadly quiet. "I said I'm not going with you."

She turned and walked out of the room and up the stairs to her bedroom, where she managed, though not without great effort, not to slam the door behind herself. She didn't see any more of him, after that. In fact, when she emerged an hour later, Robert was nowhere to be seen. But, the door to his room was firmly closed, and she breathed a sigh of relief. They just had to get through the night, and then he would leave— on his own, without them.

Late that evening, Hugh rang her cell phone to see if everything was still all right, and she admitted that Robert was spending the night in the house with them, but would be leaving in the morning. She thought it best to be honest with him, just in case.

His reaction was what she expected it to be. "Really?" he sarcastically asked. "I just want to be sure that I have this straight. You really allowed this man, a possible smuggler, to spend the night in that house with you and the girls and that padlocked room. Am I right? Or, am I having a bad dream?"

Zoe was dead-tired, and she leaned back against her pillows. She had brought a novel along, and was attempting to read it.

"Don't do this," she warned Hugh. "What was I supposed to do? He showed up at the door because my Jeep is obviously parked out front, and then he announced that he would stay the night. Should I have told him, 'No, you can't stay here because I, and a local deputy, think that you're a thief and a smuggler?' "

"He's leaving in the morning," she repeated, and then added, "Robert also demanded that we leave with him in the morning, and I refused. I'm doing the best I can with a bad situation, Hugh. Just get off my back and leave me alone. I don't really need to answer to you, about this."

The anger drained out of him, and his voice was gentle when he spoke. "I know. Just be careful, Zoe," he added. "Smugglers can be ruthless people; especially when they feel threatened. Now I really wish that you and Kate had just gone on home a couple of days ago." When she didn't reply, he sighed.

"Let me know if you need me, and be very, very careful." She

agreed and hung up. It would be a long night, but there was nothing for

it.

Chapter Twenty-Seven

Zoe poured herself a cup of coffee and sat down. She felt both exhausted and relieved, and was considering what she could do with the girls that day, when they entered the kitchen and pulled out the chairs nearest hers.

"Mom," Kate asked, "Is Robert gone?"

"It looks that way," Zoe answered. "He probably needed to leave early and didn't want to wake us up," she added. There was no need for Kate to know that Robert had expected them to leave when he did.

"Sarah," Zoe changed the subject. "What did your dad say about those coins you found? Did you get a chance to show them to him?"

"I did," she answered, "and he said he didn't know what they were, but said that he would research them and let me know. But," she asked, "Did you find out what they were?"

"I think so," Zoe brushed her hand across her forehead. "I think they're Syrian, though it would be interesting to know what something like that is doing here in the Outer Banks."

"They probably belong to a collector, Mom," Kate frowned. "But, wouldn't a collector be really careful not to lose something like that? I mean, it's not like the kind of thing that people just carry around in their pockets, is it?"

For a moment, Zoe was tempted to confide in her daughter. Young as she was, maybe Kate deserved to know what Hugh and she suspected, and perhaps her awareness might even help them, somehow. On the other hand, she could hardly tell Kate about their suspicions in front of Sarah. In the end, Zoe decided to talk to her the next time they had a few minutes alone.

After breakfast, the girls collected their school books and returned to the kitchen table, where Zoe left them working. The day passed quietly, with intermittent walks along the shore followed by rounds of hot chocolate. Late in the afternoon, Sarah wanted to go home to see if her dad had turned up anything about the Syrian coins.

"I'm going along; okay, Mom?" Kate asked. "Should I take Woolf with me?"

"No," Zoe shook her head. "He was outside, not too long ago. But," she added, "be back here before dark." She frowned. "Would you feel safer with Woolf with you?"

"Sarah's dad doesn't like him too well, so maybe I'll leave him here," Kate decided. "We won't be gone very long, anyway." Little did

she know how wrong that statement would prove to be.

Chapter Twenty-Eight

When Zoe next looked at the clock, nearly two hours had passed and the sun was going down, and the girls still hadn't returned. She had felt unexplainably uneasy all afternoon, but had kept busy, and the time had seemed to her to pass quickly. But she couldn't help feeling the way she did. Zoe told herself that the girls were, no doubt, playing at Sarah's house, and would surely return soon.

Finally, a half-hour later, she gave it up and decided to telephone to insist that Kate come home right away, and to bring Sarah with her, if possible. But first, Zoe pulled on her emerald-green sweater and crossed the room for one more look out the window. Violet-red streaks of color overlaid the late-afternoon golden blue. And, there was still no sign of the girls.

She rang Steve's number several times, but no one answered, which alarmed her even more. Surely he hadn't taken the girls somewhere and then failed to tell her about it. Well, she couldn't wait any longer; she had to get to Sarah's house as quickly as possible and see what was going on. She decided that she would just tell him that dinner was ready, and that Kate needed to come home with her.

Zoe ran upstairs to grab her cell phone. As she snatched it from the top of the dresser, she noticed something else. There, beside her phone, lay a small stack of coins that she had earlier removed from her wallet. But, one of them, the one on top, looked exactly like those that Sarah and Kate had found at the shore and close to the house.

Zoe dropped her phone and fished the photocopy of Sarah's coin out of her pocket. She was right; they were the same. In fact, they were identical. She sank down on the edge of her bed and covered her face with her hands. What did it mean? Who had placed that Syrian coin on her dresser? An overwhelming feeling rose up in her, that she, that they, were being baited by someone.

She decided that it had to have been Robert. He had been the only other person in the house. Or, had he? Was it possible that the girls had picked up more than two coins? But, why would they have laid one of them on her dresser without telling her? Was it meant to be a warning, instead? She reminded herself that even if the coin was part of a smuggled cache, the girls wouldn't know that, and neither would she. So, had Robert placed it there?

As far as she knew, no one knew that she, and Hugh, suspected that artifacts from the Middle East were being smuggled and hidden in the locked room of her rented house. On the other hand, if someone had purposely put that coin on her dresser, then they were also purposely exposing their activities and were perhaps assuming, even hoping, that she would figure it out. She felt sure that it had been meant as a warning. Was that why Robert had insisted that she and Kate were going to leave with him?

She thrust those troubling thoughts aside. Right now, the most important thing was to find Kate. She knew that she also needed to call Hugh and explain her suspicions to him. And, she fully intended to do that. But first, she had to find Kate and bring her back to the house.

As Zoe retrieved her jacket from where it hung in the laundry-room, she tripped on the bunched-up, throw-rug that lay across the doorway. As she automatically reached down to straighten it, she noticed something gold, tucked just under the edge. She knew she should just leave it until she came back, but something compelled her to kneel down and pick up whatever the object might be. A wave of shock ran through her. The gold object was yet another Syrian coin that matched the others, and in that moment, she finally realized the absolute significance of what Sarah had said earlier—that her dad was a coin collector.

The full realization of what was happening, what must have happened, came to her with such abruptness that it literally took her breath away. She instinctively folded her hands protectively over her heart. Someone besides Robert, or maybe it was Robert, had been in the house earlier. Perhaps on the day they had gone to Manteo and had taken Woolf with them. That's what they were waiting for—for Woolf to be gone, as well. She had been a fool. And, she had briefly allowed herself to feel too safe.

"How stupid could I have been?" she asked, aloud. Her breath caught in her throat and nearly choked her. Sarah and Kate had taken the coin that Sarah had found on the beach to show to, of all people, Steve Miller. According to Sarah, he shipped all sorts of things for people. And he collected ancient coins. And, so did Robert. It was too great a coincidence.

Zoe sat down hard on the floor and Woolf ran to her and began to whimper. She gently stroked his head. "It's okay, Boy," she absent-mindedly murmured.

The coins were Syrian; she had already suspected that fact to be a dead-giveaway to the smugglers' plot. And, she had to admit that the smugglers had been clever. What better place to store and move the antiquities from, than a fairly deserted and partially inaccessible section of the North Carolina shore. It was perfect—even she could see that.

In fact, the whole set-up was so reasonable that it stunned her. "But," she asked herself, "Why did Robert rent the house to me if it was used as a place to store the artifacts?" She shook her head. "There must be more than coins or other artifacts involved because they certainly wouldn't need an entire room to hold coins in. There has to be more."

Perhaps Robert hadn't realized that whatever was stored in the house had not been moved off the property when he arranged to rent it to her, she reasoned. Surely, smugglers must work to some sort of schedule. In spite of her sudden, twin-desires to break down the door to the locked room, and to call Hugh as quickly as possible, she needed to find Kate first. Any delay could be dangerous. She would call him as soon as she returned, and let him decide what to do.

In her haste, Zoe didn't think to lock the door. She slammed it behind herself, leaving an irate, barking Woolf behind.

Chapter Twenty-Nine

It felt like it took forever to run through the sand, but not too much later, Zoe knocked on Steve Miller's door and then walked in without waiting for him to answer it. She stopped abruptly. He was leaning against the dining-room door-frame, and stared at her as she threw open his front door and rushed in. Her eyes darted around the room, looking for the girls, and she saw Kate sitting quietly, with her hands folded, on an old, flowered couch with Sarah huddled close beside her. Both girls turned to look at her. Their eyes were large and frightened, and held a mute appeal for help. Steve neither spoke nor moved. But, he looked thoughtfully from one to the other of them.

Zoe's mind was racing. What was going on? Was Steve simply irritated because she'd burst into his house? She decided that it would be wise to act as though nothing was wrong, and she even managed to paste a thin smile on her face. What she didn't realize, was that fear was also written there. And, Steve saw it.

"You all are awfully quiet," Zoe attempted to sound casual. Without waiting for a response, she said, "Dinner is ready at home and I just came to fetch Kate, and to see if Sarah wanted to come back again, too. Is that okay with you?"

Steve stared at her. She cleared her throat and tried again. "Is it okay if she comes back with us? Maybe she could spend the night, again."

Steve still didn't answer. He looked as though he was trying to make up his mind about something.

"If only I'd brought Woolf along," Zoe realized. But, it was too late now.

She was on her own, and she had to do whatever she could. She straightened her shoulders, pushed back her hair and attempted to sound more brisk and confident. "Well, it's time to come home now, Kate. Wouldn't you like to come too, Sarah?"

Steve broke his long silence with a snort, and she involuntarily jumped. "Um…it's not quite that simple, is it?" He stood up straight and folded his arms. "You've guessed, haven't you?" he asked.

Zoe asked, "What do you mean? Guessed what?" She stepped directly in front of him.

"What do you think I mean?" he snarled back at her.

"Look…" she began, but he stopped her.

"Look yourself, you stupid woman," he spat out his words. "You couldn't just get out of that house like any normal person would have done, could you? God knows that Robert and I both tried, but you just wouldn't leave! What the hell is wrong with you?" He threw his arms in the air.

"Dad," a whisper escaped Sarah's lips, as she stood up and went to him. "Please, just let it go. Just this once, please. I'll never ask you for anything else, ever," she pleaded, as tears began to roll down her pale cheeks.

Steve gave her an appraising look. "Is that what you want?" he asked.

"Yes," she gulped, hopefully.

Suddenly, he reached out and slapped her face so quickly that she couldn't have guessed it was coming. She crumpled on the floor.

"Ah...too bad, Sarah," he said. "Sorry, can't help you. However, I will give you permission to go along with your friends, because we're all going for a ride together. Now."

Horrified, Zoe pulled Sarah to her feet. "But, your own daughter...." She got no farther before Steve cut her off. "But, she's not my own daughter, surely she's told you that by now. Her mother was also a pale, scared semblance of a human being, just like her."

"I did try to leave her out of this, though," he nodded to where Sarah had pulled herself up and sat, openly sobbing, on the floor. "But, no, Sarah, it was just too much to think that you could mind your own business and let me take care of mine. I can't risk you spilling the beans to someone, someday."

Steve strode across the room as he spoke, and picked up a handgun that was lying on a table near the door. Zoe hadn't noticed it, but then she had only had eyes for the girls. She wondered if they had known that it was there.

"Okay," Steve ordered, "Get your coats. Wouldn't want you to catch cold on your way to die." He chuckled at the irony of his cruel joke, then shouted, "Come on, Robert! It's time to quit hiding and time to act like the man you've never been!"

As he spoke, his eyes never left the three of them, now standing huddled together with Sarah's small, bruised face buried in the side of Zoe's coat. Zoe audibly gasped as Robert walked down the stairs and into the room with a sheepish look on his face, and the inability to meet their eyes. Instead, he looked at the floor as he spoke.

"Look, Zoe and Kate, I never intended for this to happen to you. I really thought that the artifacts were already out of the house when I brought you down here. Then," he shrugged his shoulders and looked up, "you wouldn't leave when we tried to scare you out. No—you had to become friends with that nosy, local deputy and, of course, Woolf always did make you feel safer than you really were. I really tried to get you to leave with me this morning. If only you had, you'd all be safe now."

Robert leaned back against the wall, and folded his arms across his chest. "Well...I'm sorry but neither your dog nor the deputy can help you now. Zoe, I want you to know though, that I really did care for you. I might even have married you."

"What? Without my consent?" she shot back with sudden fire in her green eyes.

His face reddened and he took a step toward her. For a moment, she wondered if he might slap her. But, instead, with visible effort, he regained control of his temper, and shrugged. "It is what it is."

"Pretension always was your strongest asset, Robert," she sarcastically observed.

Steve, still holding the gun in his hand, gestured at the girls to put on their coats. "Okay, enough," he said. "Tie their hands with this rope, Robert, and let's get out of here."

Robert fumbled with the ropes until Steve finally lost patience and handed him the gun. "Here, I'll do it myself. Honestly, are you good for anything?" he muttered.

"Good enough to help you get what you want," Robert retorted. "Don't forget..." But, Steve interrupted him. "Yeah, okay. Let's just get them out of here."

Steve tied the ropes around their wrists tightly and somewhat painfully, and Zoe realized that the chances of wriggling out of them were poor-to-nonexistent. "Okay, let's go," he ordered. The girls led the way and Zoe followed with Steve close behind and his gun pushing against her back.

It was quiet outside and dark now, though the moonlight was bright whenever it chanced to break through the passing clouds. Only the distant sound of frantic barking broke the star-studded silence. It was Woolf, frantic to get to them and unable to do so. As the little group reached Steve's SUV, he paused to tell them, "It's no use screaming. No one will hear you and I will shoot you dead before you can close your mouths. And, that's a promise."

Incredibly, the next moment found them frozen in their respective positions. "It just can't be," thought Zoe," but it is." Sure enough, it was Susan Hill who was shouting and waving as she approached them. Steve whispered at the back of Zoe's head, "Don't even think about it, or she'll be coming along with us."

Susan, who seemed to be completely oblivious to what was happening, called out, "Hello, dears," in her typically cheerful voice. "It looks like you're on your way out. Are you going out for dinner together, somewhere?"

The moment of silence that followed was abruptly broken by Robert. "No, we're just going out for a drive. It's such a pretty night, don't you think?"

He smiled at her. "Maybe we'll get some ice cream," he added, as he vaguely gestured toward the vehicle.

Susan responded, "How nice," and pushed her way past the men until she stood directly in front of Zoe. The older woman chattered on about her own favorite brand of ice cream, and the weather, and her favorite local restaurants. And, although she seemed to include all of them in her conversation, her eyes locked directly onto Zoe's. She sounded as vague as ever, but in that moment, Zoe realized that there was nothing vague about the woman. Susan's eyes were, in fact, quite shrewd and intelligent.

The conversation was one-sided; they were clearly waiting for Susan to leave. But, with all her heart, Zoe willed the older woman to understand her unspoken plea for help and a part of her felt certain that Susan had understood. Or, had she? Zoe wondered if she was seeing help where there was none, because she was so desperate.

In the end, Susan nodded slightly at Zoe and then abruptly waved good-bye to everyone and wished them a good evening. She didn't' look back, though Zoe half-hoped that she would. As soon as the older woman was out of sight, Steve stuck the gun against Zoe's back once again, and ordered them all into the back seat of his SUV. Hopelessly, the girls huddled, one on each side of Zoe, seeking the protection that she could not offer them. Over and outside the fear, she ached for them. They were so young. She had to think—if only there was one man instead of two to deal with. But, there were two, and one of them had a gun. And, she had no doubt that he would use it.

As they drove, Zoe looked out into the night, scanning the sky as though the solution to their problems might lay hidden somewhere in the stars, and wondered if this would really be their last night on earth. It certainly seemed so. She unconsciously raised her head and lifted her chin. "Well," she determined, "I'm not going out without a fight. Maybe an idea will present itself, yet."

At that moment, Kate looked up at her with pleading eyes. "Mommy," she whispered; a name she hadn't called her mother in a very long time. Zoe nodded at her and glanced at the men. Kate took that as a warning and didn't attempt to say anything more. Sarah was quiet, and kept her face buried in the folds of Zoe's coat.

Zoe forced herself to focus. What were the possibilities? Could she just open the door and throw herself out of the vehicle? If she was fast enough, she might be able to run for help. The darkness would make it hard for the men to see her, and if she could make it as far as the wilderness of low-growing trees and brush that hugged the sand, she might have a chance of finding help. But, that would mean leaving the girls alone. She had no doubt that at least one of the men would chase her, because it was too dangerous for them to let her go.

On the other hand, she had no idea where she and the girls were being taken. Which meant that, even if she got away long enough to find help, how would they ever find the girls, again? There was also the possibility that Steve might just go ahead and shoot the girls before coming after her. No, it was too much of a risk.

Zoe was somewhat relieved when the SUV climbed up through the sand and gripped solid pavement on the Corolla Road. That hopefully meant that they weren't being put aboard a boat, which was another possibility that she had feared. Maybe something would happen; maybe Susan had gone for help, after all.

She was also struggling with the idea that Robert was a part of this, and she wondered if she might be able to reason with him. "Robert…," she ventured.

But, without turning his head, he raised one hand to silence her and said, "Oh, shut up, Zoe. It'll soon be over, now." His voice sounded flat and tired, and she wondered if, perhaps, he hadn't understood that his smuggling activities might include having to commit murder.

Soon, much too soon, Steve pulled into a parking lot near the old Currituck Lighthouse, whose guiding beam had broken the darkness for over 100 years.

As he turned off the ignition, she peered through the front window from her seat in the back, and bluntly asked, "What are you going to do to us?" The men looked at each other, but it was Steve who answered.

"I guess it doesn't matter if we tell you, now." He grinned at Robert, who did not return the gesture. "In fact, I'll think of it as your final request," Steve smirked.

"See that stretch of dirt piled up over there?" He pointed and shone a flashlight toward a lengthy stretch of mounded-up earth. "A new water-line was run through there recently and now, the county intends to put the dirt back in and plant shrubbery over it. But, I figure that it will serve just as well for three graves because it's pretty deep, you know."

He was clearly enjoying discussing his plans to her. "We're going to stash you on the far end over there, put some shrubs over you, and push in enough dirt to literally plant you." He paused to chuckle at his own, cruel joke.

"Once the county boys see a few bushes in the ground, they'll be happy to just pick up where we left off. But, I'll bet the bushes where you're planted will grow even better than the others. I'll have to keep an eye on them and see how they do." This time, he laughed heartily and then nudged Robert, who wasn't saying anything, and who wasn't laughing.

"Come on," Steve addressed Robert. "This is no time to lose your nerve. You know, man, you really need to learn how to chill more. You're much too serious." He leaned over and playfully slapped Robert's shoulder, but Robert continued to sit in silence and Steve mockingly asked, "Did you really think that smuggling was a game?"

Zoe's voice trembled, but she needed to ask. "Robert—why?"

"Why do you think?" he snapped. "For the money, of course. How can I ever afford to retire the way I want to, on the salary that I make? And, no one will probably ever suspect me. After all, I'm well-respected in our line of work, you know."

"But they will," she cried. "Sooner or later, they will suspect you and you'll be retiring to prison!"

Steve turned around and pointed the gun directly at her face. "Okay, that's enough. Let's move—all of you." All three emerged from the back seat of the vehicle and looked around themselves in desperation.

Kate faced her mother and simply said, "Mom."

"Honey," Zoe leaned over and kissed the top of her daughter's head, "we love each other. "Whatever happens to us will never change that. At least these sorry excuses for human beings don't have the power to take that away from us," she added defiantly.

Tears ran down Kate's cheeks as she said, "And, at least we'll be together with Dad, again,"

Zoe nodded and turned to Sarah. "Kate and I love you too, Sarah. Whatever happens, remember that."

"Okay, great," Steve said, as he shepherded them toward the light-house and the drainage ditch beyond. "You've said your good-byes and now we can just get on with this." Abruptly, the unexpected howl of sirens shattered the silent night. At first, the sound was not close, but it steadily grew louder. Zoe's heart raced. It was for them—it had to be someone coming to help them. Susan must have gone to the police, after all.

She wondered what she could do to delay Steve's plans long enough for the police to find them. The other immediate problem was how to make sure that the police were able to see where they were. The lighthouse was partially surrounded by what appeared to be acres of trees and undergrowth, the thickest part of which faced the road. Her hands were bound; there was no way to grab the flashlight that Robert was holding.

Just at that moment, another sound became apparent to all of them. It was the pounding sound of a galloping horse. None of them could tell which direction the sound was coming from, but, like the sirens, the galloping was also coming closer.

Both men were distracted, particularly by the sound of the horse, and Zoe

quietly ordered the girls to go stand close against the brick-wall of the

lighthouse, where she placed herself between them. But, Robert and Steve did

not pay much attention. Although Steve continued to point the gun at them, his

eyes were not on them. Instead, he was looking around with a bewildered

expression on his face.

Robert moved closer to him and had just whirled around for the second

time, trying to see where the sound was coming from, when a white stallion

broke through the darkness. He ran straight at them, moving so fast that there

was no time for anyone to react. A faint glow of light surrounded him. But the

most unnerving sight was that of the wildness in his eyes. His teeth were bared,

and his ears laid back.

Kate shouted, "The Ghost Horse! It's the Ghost Horse!" But if it was the

Ghost Horse, his form appeared to be every bit as solid as those of his earthly

counterparts.

Panicked, Robert turned to bolt. But before he gained more than a

couple of strides, the horse seized the back of his collar, easily lifted him off the

ground, and hurled him into the side of the brick lighthouse, close to where Zoe

and the girls stood. The blow left him crumpled on the ground like a broken,

abandoned doll.

Steve, who had run in the opposite direction, turned and fired a couple of shots at the horse. Quick bursts of fire from the gun's barrel lit the darkness as both Kate and Sarah screamed and then abruptly stopped. Either Steve had completely missed his target, or the bullets had been unable to pierce the horse. What they did do though, was to draw the mustang's attention away from Robert and toward Steve.

The two of them, man and horse, eyed each other for a long moment. The horse appeared to be fixing his next target, and Steve knew it. He completely lost his nerve, tossed his gun in the air, and ran for all he was worth. But, of course, the horse was faster and easily ran him down. The powerful front hooves crashed into the back of the fleeing man and threw him to the ground. The breath was knocked out of him, and Steve was unable to rise. But, it wouldn't have mattered, anyway. The mustang was too quick for him. With no hesitation, the horse reared on his hind legs and drove his weight directly into the man's back, crushing him. And Steve did not move, again.

The horse lowered his head and touched the dead man with his nose, perhaps to be certain that he was no longer a threat. Then, he walked to where Robert still lay, unconscious, and whinnied softly to himself before turning his magnificent face toward Zoe and the girls. Time stood still as their eyes met and held until, finally, Kate broke the silence.

"It was us you came to help, after all!" she called to him. "Thank you for saving us." She pushed away from the wall to go to him, but the stallion whinnied loudly, and she stopped. He raised his face to the sky, shook out his silvery mane, and faded.

Chapter Thirty

Time resumed once more. Shouting replaced the sound of sirens, as Hugh and another uniformed officer ran toward them with their guns drawn. Ahead of them ran Woolf, whose wild barking drowned whatever words the men were shouting. The dog reached Steve, first. He flung himself at the body, but at the smell of death, he stopped and whimpered, instead.

He sniffed Robert, then, he ran to where Kate now knelt in the damp grass. His bark was sharp and excited, and she longed to throw her arms around his neck and bury her face in his thick fur. His comfort was that of home and belonging, and she needed him.

Both officers shoved their guns back into their holsters, and Hugh ran to cut the ropes that bound the captives' wrists, while the other officer knelt and examined first one man, then the other. Once Zoe and the girls were freed, Hugh reached for his phone and called for an ambulance. The other officer took off his jacket and tucked it around Robert's shoulders. "This looks pretty serious to me," he said. "At the very least, it's a concussion, but there might be internal injuries, too."

Hugh spared a moment to briefly look at Steve, then hurried back to where Zoe, the girls, and Woolf, waited together.

"Thank God you're safe," he panted. "You're alright! If we'd been any later…." He impulsively threw his arms around Zoe, nearly suffocating her in his heavy jacket. When he finally released her, he kept one arm tightly around her shoulders as he ruffled each of the girls' hair in turn, with his free hand.

"Are you two okay?" he asked. "Did they hurt you at all?" Without waiting for an answer, he added, "We'd better get you checked out at the hospital just to make sure."

Zoe surprised herself by clinging as tightly to him, as he was clinging to her. "Honestly," she told him, "the last thing I want to do right now, is to sit in a hospital emergency room. Please just take us home. We're okay; we just want to go home, Hugh." Her voice cracked.

"But, don't you think…" he began, and she interrupted. "No. I don't. The good news is that they didn't have a chance to really hurt us." Then, in spite of her efforts, she began to cry.

"They were smuggling coins, and maybe other artifacts, out of the Middle East," she sobbed, then took a deep breath and steadied herself. "I'll tell you all about it. But Hugh, they were going to kill us and bury us in that drainage ditch." Her voice broke again, and Hugh pulled out a folded handkerchief and passed it to her.

The other office stood up and walked over to them, and Hugh interrupted her. "Believe me, Zoe, I intend to hear everything you have to say. But first," he gestured at the other man, "this is Aaron. He's a good man, and he's also one of the squad's sharp-shooters. He's on duty tonight, and I'm sure glad that he is. I was afraid that we might need his skills, given the circumstances."

Aaron stepped forward and took Zoe's hand. "Are you all alright, Ma'am? And are those girls alright?"

"Yes," she answered, "thanks to…" she hesitated, not quite sure how to explain what had just happened. She nodded in the direction of the two fallen men. "But, what about them?" One of them had begun to moan.

Aaron pointed at Robert. "That one may have some broken bones and probably a concussion. We're getting him to the hospital; an ambulance is on its way."

He gestured toward Steve. "That one, is dead. As near as I can tell…" he hesitated, "well, to tell you the truth, ma'am, he looks like he tangled with one of the wild mustangs hereabouts. There are wet, sandy hoof-prints in the wounds on his back."

Aaron looked thoughtfully at the ground, then lifted his eyes to Zoe's. "But that doesn't make any sense," He frowned. "Are you able to explain what happened to him?"

"This," he continued, and gestured at the body, "doesn't make any sense to me. What I can't figure out, is why would a horse have attacked him right here and now, and tonight? Don't get me wrong," he explained, "there's a reason why you don't mess with the wild horses, but they generally leave you alone unless you provoke them and they think you're a threat. They don't just randomly attack without a good reason." He shook his head.

Kate, who had little patience with her mother's disbelief in the miraculous, looked up and declared, "It was the Ghost Horse. You should have seen him," she said. "He went right for them and then Steve shot at him, but of course, you can't shoot a ghost, can you?" She looked up at Hugh in order to gauge whether or not he believed her.

To her relief, Hugh smiled back and shook his head. "No, Kate, you can't shoot a ghost." He reached over and patted her shoulder.

At that moment, they were interrupted by the arrival of two ambulances, with sirens blaring and lights flashing. Hugh released Zoe, and he and Aaron hurried over to the EMS crews. In the quiet that followed, Zoe walked back over to the lighthouse and leaned against the solid brick. She folded her arms and looked up to where the stars shone brightly in some places and were obscured in others. She considered them, and said to the girls. "Isn't the sky a wonder?" They looked up.

"What you see there is just like life, isn't it?" she reflected. "Some of it you see clearly and it sparkles. Other aspects of it are obscure, and you have to find your way through the clouds until you reach the bits that sparkle clearly, again." The girls didn't answer, nor did she expect them to.

"What's going to happen to me now?" Sarah whispered as she went to stand close against Zoe.

Zoe bent down, rested her hand on the child's shoulder, and asked, "Do you have any other family, Sarah? Any grandparents, aunts or uncles?" Sarah shook her head and fresh tears began to course down her cheeks.

"Sarah," Zoe said firmly, "Listen to me." Sarah raised her eyes and met Zoe's. "You will come and live with us. Hugh will help us figure it all out. But, you will be my daughter and Kate will be your sister. Is that okay? Would you like that?"

"Oh, yes," Sarah threw herself into Zoe's arms and Kate came to pat her back. "It'll be fun, Sarah. Woolf and I have always wanted a sister," she gently teased.

Not long after, the ambulances pulled away and Hugh and Aaron hurried back to them. Aaron, especially, seemed unsure about what to do next. Obviously, they would need to take statements, but neither was looking forward to reporting that the injury and death was a result of a ghostly manifestation, and specifically that of a horse. They knew how that would go down at headquarters.

Both men looked inquiringly at Zoe, who glanced at Kate and Sarah. She pushed herself away from the wall and stood up straight, as Hugh went to her and put his arm around her, again.

"I will tell you exactly what I saw happen, gentlemen," she said, "and I swear that it is the truth. Do you understand that? I am going to tell you the truth," she repeated. Defensively, she pulled away from Hugh. Her words were a challenge to both men, and she was daring them to disbelieve what she was about to say.

"The absolute truth is what Kate already told you. I swear, a galloping, white horse came out of nowhere and attacked these men. And then," she added, "it disappeared. Look, you saw this for yourselves. You saw the hoof-prints. Explain to me how-on-earth it could have happened otherwise," she insisted. Neither man could think of anything to say.

Tiredness suddenly overwhelmed her, and Zoe was no longer defiant, but achingly tired, instead. She lifted her arms in frustration and said, "That's what happened, boys; take it or leave it. And now, I want to go home. We," she corrected herself, "want to go home."

Hugh's voice was gentle. He glanced at Aaron before meeting her eyes. "I believe you," he said.

Aaron nodded in agreement. "I do, too, to tell you the truth. And, in spite of the fact that I don't believe in ghosts. But," he added, "I would really like to hear more of the details. I think we can wrap this up for now, though. We'll talk again tomorrow. Just let us know if you remember anything different or important, at any point."

Chapter Thirty-One

They all headed back to the parking lot, and as Aaron got into his car and pulled away, Hugh shepherded Zoe and the girls into his own squad car. "In you go, girls, and you too, Woolf." He leaned on the top of the open door as they climbed into the back seat. Then, he held the passenger door for Zoe. The trip back was quiet. Everyone was exhausted and grateful, and for the time being, that was enough.

Although only a couple of hours had passed since Zoe and the girls had been driven to what was meant to be their deaths, Zoe found herself looking around as though the sight of the ocean and the sand-dunes were new to her. She admitted to herself that she'd come to believe that she wouldn't be seeing any of it, ever again.

In the back seat, Kate sat as closely to Woolf as possible, and rested her head against his, while Sarah huddled close against his other side. Neither spoke.

Impulsively, Zoe lowered her window and turned to them to explain. "I know it's chilly outside, but I just have to smell the wind and feel it on my face."

Hugh reached over and squeezed her hand. "The sweet smell of freedom; am I right?" he asked.

She nodded, not trusting herself to speak. Unexpected tears had welled up in her eyes, again.

Kate's thoughts were neither on the beach nor on the salty, night air, nor on the miracle of returning back to the house, alive. She had sat back up, because it had occurred to her that the Ghost Horse might be standing somewhere along the shore. Surely, since he had just saved their lives, he would appear again. At least, one more time. But, the beach remained empty. Misty clouds continued to drift across the opal moon, as cold wind rippled the ocean's depths.

Kate felt that she had to see the horse again, even if it was for the last time. Suddenly, she felt a strange sense of isolation from everything else. There was only the ocean, the stars and moon, and the wind. They might be the only people left on earth. "It's just this night and everything that's happened," she thought to herself, as she watched the rising mist roll in. "It feels spooky. But, maybe that means that the Horse will come again, after all."

As they pulled up to the house, Hugh glanced over at Zoe. "Do you want to know how I found out what was happening to you?" He stopped his car just short of the car-port roof, and turned off the engine.

She shook her head. "I hadn't thought anymore about it, to tell you the truth. I guess I'm still just so relieved to be safe. Was it Susan?" she asked. He seemed surprised. "Susan Hill called me," he confirmed. "Would you like to hear about it?"

"Yes, I would," Zoe said. "But first, do any of you want some hot chocolate?" Without waiting for an answer, she added, "Never mind; I'm going to make some anyway. We're all cold and need some comfort."

A minute later, she flipped on the familiar, kitchen light and assembled what she needed. As she stood stirring cocoa and sugar into hot milk on the stove, she marveled at how normal it felt to do that, and was grateful. It was amazing how much the small things of life meant to her in that moment.

The girls went upstairs to change into pajamas, and Hugh turned on the gas fireplace, then came in and pulled a chair back from the table. She turned and looked expectantly at him, then explained.

"Okay, in answer to your question, Susan saw us leaving Steve's house. She pushed her way over to me and looked directly into my eyes, and I kept hoping that she understood that we were in trouble, and that she would go for help."

Zoe pulled her sweater more tightly around herself and continued. "I am ashamed to say that when I looked at her, I mean really looked at her, I realized that there really is nothing vague about her, at all."

Hugh folded his arms and leaned back. "I could have told you that, if you'd only been willing to listen to me. She comes across as a little scatty." Zoe raised her eyebrows in response, but he ignored the gesture.

"But, believe me," he continued, "she is not. Furthermore, she's a good person, Zoe. And, there is no doubt that she saved your life, tonight," he added.

"Helped save our lives," she corrected him. "I'm serious about that horse, Hugh." She leaned across the table. "I know what I saw, and he came to help us. He went right past us and after those men with no hesitation, whatsoever. I doubt they even had time to register what was happening to them."

Hugh didn't answer, and she persisted. "You can think whatever you want to think, Deputy, but I know what I know." She lifted her chin stubbornly.

Hugh sighed, and then heaved himself out of his chair, opened cupboard doors, and hunted until he located four mugs for the chocolate. "Please come and sit down here, Zoe, because we need to talk."

"In a minute," she answered. "First, I need to take care of the girls." She pulled a plastic tray that was lavishly decorated with sunflowers, from the bottom of another cupboard, and loaded the girls' cocoa onto it. She pulled graham crackers out of a plastic container, piled them onto a plate, and headed for the stairs.

The bedroom door was open, and Zoe found Kate positioned at the window, watching for the Ghost Horse, while Sarah lay in bed with the covers pulled up to her chin. Woolf lay close beside her and he didn't move to get off the bed when he saw Zoe. After all that had happened, she didn't have the heart to order him off the bed, either.

Kate turned to her. "I keep hoping that he'll come back. I mean the horse, you know. Do you think he will, Mom?"

"Yes, Honey, I do," she nodded, "or at least I hope he will, for your sake."

"Kate, I certainly can't begin to explain any of this, but I do know that I was wrong about the horse. And, I need to apologize to you for not believing you, in the first place. Now," she continued, "I realize that he was looking out for us all along. Anyway, I do think he'll come back, even if it's just to see you once more."

Kate took a mug from her mother and sat down on the edge of the bed. She was cold, and the hot stoneware felt good in her hands.

"Thanks," she said. "And, Mom? It's okay. I know that you were too scared to believe in the Ghost Horse at first, but I want you to know that it's okay." She smiled as Zoe pulled her into her arms.

"But, I am sorry, Honey. For that, and for not being able to make everything right for you, again. You're right; I've been scared, up until now. But, not anymore," she looked into Kate's eyes. "Everything is going to be okay now, Kate. I just know it will be. We all have each other," her smile included Sarah, who solemnly watched them.

She dropped a kiss on Sarah's forehead, handed her a mug, and said, "I need to get back downstairs, girls, but remember I'm right here if you need me. Don't worry," she repeated, "everything will be alright now."

Chapter Thirty-Two

Back downstairs, she settled into the kitchen chair opposite Hugh's and said, "Okay, I'm ready to have that talk with you, and," she added, "thanks for waiting patiently."

He settled back in his chair, and though he smiled at her, his eyes were solemn.

"First of all," she said, "do you know anything about the coins?" He shook his head and looked puzzled. Zoe explained how the girls had found a couple of coins, and that when she had researched them online, she'd discovered that they were ancient, Syrian coins. She went on to tell him that she'd later found a couple more of the same coins in the house, and then realized that the smugglers, themselves, had been in the house, possibly while it had been left unguarded by Woolf.

"Why-on-earth didn't you just call me?" His voice rose as he sat up straight and brought his fist down on the table.

"Because," she said, "the girls were there, in Sarah's house, and I knew that a trap had been set. We had unwittingly taken the bait. I guess that in the end, they wanted us to know, so that they could finally get rid of us."

"But, why do anything that drastic?" Hugh asked.

"Because we wouldn't leave," Zoe answered. "If we'd left with Robert this morning, as he asked us to do, then none of the rest of this would have happened. But," she added, "I didn't understand that at the time."

Hugh shook his head as she continued. "Hugh, they would have counted those coins. They would have known how many they had, and were supposed to have. Every one of those coins is valuable. Whoever set the trap for us deliberately placed the coins where they did, in order to pull us into the trap."

A shadow crossed her face. "I just thought of something. There's still someone else, or maybe a couple of people out there who are also in on this. It can't have been just the two of them, don't you think?"

Hugh reassured her. "Listen, Zoe, while you were upstairs with the girls, Aaron called to tell me that Robert is conscious. In spite of the fact that he does have a concussion, he has been spilling the beans about everything he knows, as fast as he can. He is hoping that if he cooperates, his prison sentence will be reduced. He might be a crook, but he's not a loyal one, thankfully."

"As a result," he went on, "officers have been dispatched locally, and customs authorities are being alerted, as are some government officials. As of about 15-minutes ago, the two other local people who are involved, were arrested."

He rubbed his chin. "I have no doubt that Robert will spill everything he knows about his contacts in the Middle East, too."

Zoe sighed and leaned back. "I am so relieved that I hardly know what to say. But," she continued, "I promised to tell you everything."

"First," she began, "Steve planned to have us lay down in the ditches, where he would shoot us. Then, he and Robert planned to bury us," she shuddered. "But, before anything actually happened, we heard the sound of a galloping horse. You know what that sounds like, don't you? We all heard it. But, you know, in the dark, it's really hard to tell where sound comes from, and none of us, including Steve and Robert, had any idea."

"It was unnerving though," she confessed, "and the sound kept coming closer. I think we all wondered if the horse was going to trample us before we could move out of the way. We heard it crashing through the trees and brush and then, suddenly, it burst into the clearing. "

"It was pretty dark, though, with the clouds coming and going," Hugh said, "especially in the shadows where you were. Were you really able to see the horse before he was on top of you? "

"That is the really strange part," she answered. "The horse we saw, well, it...it sort of glowed, Hugh. In fact, it looked sort of misty, too, but was obviously a solid being to have done what he did to those men."

"What I'll never forget, for as long as I live, was his eyes. Those eyes were not like the eyes of any living thing I've ever seen, and I can only say that I wouldn't have wanted to be the one he was after. It grabbed Robert first, picked him up by the neck of his jacket, and threw him into the side of the lighthouse. You found him there, just as he was when he fell."

"Then," she continued, "he went right for Steve, who actually fired a couple of shots at him. But, Hugh," her eyes begged him to believe her, "the shots went right through him. He was close enough that Steve couldn't have missed. Then," she hesitated, reliving the scene, "the horse just ran him down. Pounded his hooves into Steve's back, and Steve died. No one could have survived that."

"Do you think it could have possibly been a horse that just attacked for some reason?" Hugh asked.

"No," she answered. "I fully believe that it was your Ghost Horse. The one you told the story about. No horse looks like that, or has eyes like that."

Hugh looked down at his hands and considered what she had said. When he spoke again, his voice was gentle. "I believe you, Zoe. Just like I believed the old man who told me that story about the Ghost Horse, years ago. He did appear when you needed him, and he did save your life. Nobody can argue that."

He cleared his throat and continued. "You know, I believe that there's a whole lot more to life than what's in front of our eyes."

"Well, after this, I certainly believe the same thing," Zoe said. "There's no way to think otherwise. And now," her voice became more brisk, "there are a few other things I have to say."

"I suppose it's never easy for anyone to admit being wrong, or being weak in any way, but I will freely admit to you now, that I was wrong about Susan Hill. I see how easy it is to misjudge someone, just because they're different. And, you're right; I had no good reason to be angry with her, in the first place. I don't even know why; I guess I was a little afraid of her."

Hugh covered her hand with his, and she shook her head.

"The truth is, up until now, it's been hard for me to believe in anything that isn't purely physical. My thought was that only fools have the luxury of believing in something that might not be real, and I felt that I couldn't afford to do that. To even consider it, because otherwise, I might agonize over where my late husband is now, and whether or not he knows what is happening to Kate and me. I've been afraid to believe, to raise my hopes falsely, to think that he still exists, only just somewhere else. Maybe heaven," she added, hopefully.

"The thing is," Zoe continued, "I couldn't bear it if I was wrong; if I was lying to myself. If I believed what Susan Hill, and you, were saying about the

Ghost Horse, then I might also have to believe that anything is possible, and maybe it isn't...wasn't," she corrected herself.

Hugh shrugged. "It's okay to be afraid sometimes, Zoe, only you can't live there, if you know what I mean. You just do the best you can, and keep faith that what you believe is right, unless you're shown otherwise. I guess you could say that we all have to live by faith. Otherwise, what else is there besides the empty darkness?"

"Well, I'm a believer now," she repeated. "What I'm having trouble with, is forgiving myself for not believing Kate when she told me that she had seen the horse. In fact, maybe it was the thought of the horse, even more than that of Susan Hill, that really frightened me," she considered.

"I understand," Hugh answered. "I've been through a few things in my time, and have been afraid to believe, too, sometimes." He took a deep breath. "And, now, I want to talk to you about something else."

Zoe looked apprehensive.

"No more bad news," he grinned. "At least not tonight, anyway. Before I go there, though, I have to tell you that Woolf really raised a ruckus. Even if Susan hadn't called, someone would have, because he was in the process of tearing down the door. In fact, you haven't had a chance to look at it yet, but I guarantee that some trim-board, and possibly the front door, will need to be replaced before you leave," his eyes twinkled.

"Hey, I'll help you out with that, though. It's nothing I can't take care of for you," he quickly added, "so don't worry about it."

"Poor Woolf," Zoe replied. "I'll never leave him like that again, at least not when I'm about to do something dangerous or stupid, or maybe both. Though I'm not planning to ever do something that desperate again," she quickly added.

Hugh said, "I asked Susan if he was with you, and she said he wasn't, but she heard him frantically barking. I came back here and grabbed him, because I figured that if we had trouble finding you, he wouldn't. He'd know where to go, even if I needed to turn him loose to do it. But, there was no leaving Woolf behind, anyway," he explained.

"He wasn't having any part of staying in the house, and I honestly think he'd have broken the door apart and taken off after you. In fact, the closer we got to the lighthouse, the more agitated he became. So, I knew we were on the right track. Meanwhile, I'd called for back-up and Aaron was on duty, as you already know."

Hugh sighed. "And now, there's another thing that you should know," his tone grew serious. "I need to admit to you that it wasn't just Woolf. I saw the horse, myself, but at first I thought it was some kind of a light."

Zoe's eyes widened, and he went on. "But, I did see it, just momentarily before he faded away. You know, maybe he waited; maybe he wanted us all to see him so that we wouldn't doubt each other, because, frankly, I think that I needed to know about him, first-hand, too."

He shrugged his shoulders and said, "The thing is, I just want you and Kate to know that I did see it after all."

Zoe started to speak, but he interrupted her. "Don't look so worried, please. That's the end of it. I'll notify Graham Owens in the morning, and everything should be okay now."

He sat up straighter. "You're safe," he said abruptly, "So, there's no more bad news, or at least I hope you don't think it's bad news. But," he continued, "I have to tell you something else, because it's important. At least it is to me.

He reached across the table and took her hand in his. "The truth is, Zoe, I've come to care for you a lot. You and Kate and Woolf. And Sarah, too," he quickly added, "because I would imagine that you're planning to keep her."

She shook her head, and he pleaded, "Listen to me for just a minute, okay? Zoe, I don't know what I'd have done if anything had happened to you and Kate. I know it's probably too soon to say such things, but...."

Zoe interrupted him. "Yes, Hugh; it is too soon, right now, tonight. But, it won't always be. Before long, it won't be." She took a deep breath. "Do you understand? Meanwhile," she continued, "we can get to know each other better, especially now that we're free from the mystery of this house. We can just start over, and then we'll see where it takes us." She looked down at their entwined hands.

Hugh gently lifted her chin. "Yes, I do understand. I understand that there is hope for us, and that's all I need to know, for now."

She smiled at the intense expression in his eyes. "If there's one thing I have learned, it's that there is always hope." He moved to the chair next to hers, and put his arms around her. She laid her head on his shoulder as he drew her close and kissed her forehead.

Chapter Thirty-Three

While her mother and Hugh were in the kitchen, Kate managed to slip down the stairs, accompanied by Woolf, and unnoticed by either of the adults. Sarah was asleep, and Kate felt that she urgently needed to go out and look for the Ghost Horse, on her own.

She quietly slipped out the front door, grateful that the hinges didn't squeak, and walked quickly toward the sea. Thick mist swirled around her, but she felt her way toward the shore where the waves quietly lapped the sand. A high, bright moon shone behind the mist, and an occasional glimpse of it helped light her way.

When Kate reached the shore, she stood quietly and waited, looking around as best she could, convinced that she would be able to see the glow of the ghostly mustang, in spite of the mist. Woolf sat protectively close to her, on the damp sand.

She soon lost track of time as she kept her stubborn vigil, watching both the sea and the sky as best she could. Then, finally, out of the corner of her eye, she saw something move. Her breath caught in her throat as that something grew clearer, and she saw that it was, indeed, the stallion, the Ghost Horse. He stood at the edge of the shore, a short distance from her, and was watching her. When he whinnied softly, she ran to where he waited.

"I'm so glad you've come," she blurted out, lest he disappear before she had a chance to say everything she wanted to say to him.

"Thank you," she said. "I'll never forget you, as long as I live. You are the most beautiful thing I've ever seen, and...and," she hesitated, "I love you." She looked into the horse's wild, unearthly eyes, and felt, beyond doubt, that he understood everything she was saying.

"Please," she continued, "if you're going away now, please come back to me again, some day. Please always come back," she pleaded with him. Tears stung her eyes. She knew he was leaving, and with her whole being, she wanted him to stay.

Kate impulsively threw out her arms and moved closer to him. She stopped in the shallow tide and glanced down as her shoes squelched in the cold, salt-water. But, when she looked up again, she saw something else in the darkness, something that was standing next to the horse. It was another shadowy figure.

She paused, waiting for her eyes to adjust, willing them to see whatever else was there. Suddenly, the mist parted so that the moonlight shone clearly. Mouth open, heart pounding furiously, she saw his smiling face. It was her father.

He did not speak, but nodded his head, as though reassuring her that everything was alright.

She longed to throw herself into his arms, but her feet wouldn't move, and she knew that she wasn't meant to move any closer to either of them. Father and daughter looked hungrily at one another across the short distance of water.

Finally, David, her father, reached toward the stallion and laid his hand on the horse's proud neck, and they both faded. Kate cried out in despair, but then, an unexplainable flash of joy and warmth swept over and through her. And, in that moment, she knew that everything really was as it should be.

She also knew, beyond the shadow of a doubt, that she and her mother were protected—loved—by more than just Woolf. She basked in that warmth, that comfort that she had longed for since her father's death until, without warning, a cold nose touched her hand. It was Woolf, who was also, in his own way, reassuring her.

Through the thickening mist, her voice sang out to him. "Come on, Woolf, there's nothing to worry about anymore." She caressed his head. "Let's go home."

Made in the USA
Middletown, DE
25 June 2023

33291733R00135